JANE HARDSTAFF

The
Executioner's
Daughter

EGMONT

EGMONT

We bring stories to life

First published in Great Britain 2014
by Egmont UK Limited, The Yellow Building,
1 Nicholas Road, London W11 4AN

Text copyright © 2014 Jane Hardstaff
Chapter illustrations © 2014 Joe McLaren

The moral rights of the author and illustrator have been asserted

ISBN 978 1 4052 6828 8

1 3 5 7 9 10 8 6 4 2

A CIP catalogue record for this title is available from the British
Library

Printed and bound in Great Britain by the CPI Group

55847/1

For Mum and Dad

Contents

CHAPTER ONE
Basket Girl

She'd never get used to beheadings. No matter what Pa said.

Peering through the arrow-slit window, Moss tried to catch a glimpse of the fields beyond Tower Hill. All she could see were people. Crazy people. Spilling out of the city. Scrabbling up the hill for the best view of the scaffold. Laughing and shouting and fighting. Madder than a sack of badgers. She could hear their cries, carried high on the wind, all the way up to the Tower.

'Get your stinking carcass off my spot!'

'Son-of-a-pikestaff, I ain't goin nowhere!'

'What are you? Dumb as a stump? Move your bum, I said! I've been camping here all night!'

'Then camp on this, coloppe-breath!'

She shook her head in disgust. Execution Days brought a frenzied crowd to Tower Hill. The more they got, the more they wanted. Like a dog with worms.

Of course, London had always been execution-mad. If there was a monk to be drawn and quartered or a Catholic to be burned, the people liked nothing better than to stand around and watch. Preferably while eating a pie. But you couldn't beat a good beheading. That's what the Tower folk said. Up on the scaffold was someone rich. Someone important. Maybe even a Royal. *That's* what people came for. Royal blood. Blood that glittered as it sprayed the crowd. It made Moss feel sick just thinking about it.

'Moss!'

Pa was calling. She could hear his cries below,

faint among the bustle on Tower Green.

'Moss, MOSS!'

He'd be panicking by now. Well, let him panic. She'd sit tight. She'd wait. With luck, he wouldn't find her. Judging by the rats' nest in the fireplace, no one had used this turret for months. No prisoners, no guards and no one to find a girl somewhere she shouldn't be.

Moss scraped her tangle-hair out of the way and pushed her freckle-face to the narrow gap. Up here, she was ten trees tall. She could see everything. On one side Tower Hill. On the other the river. And, in between, the Tower of London, planted like a giant's fist in the middle of a deep moat, lookouts knuckled on all corners. It was said that the Tower was strong enough to keep out a thousand armies. Bounded by two massive walls, it guarded the city, arrow-slit eyes trained on the river. It was a fortress, a castle and a prison. Moss had lived here all her life. And in the summer the reek of the moat made it stink like a dead dog's guts.

'Moss!'

Pa's voice was closer.

'MOSS!'

Too late she heard his feet pounding up the twist of steps. Now there was no way out. She scowled and scrunched herself into a corner.

'Are you up there?'

'No! Go away!'

His face appeared in the doorway, full of frown.

'What are you playing at? Don't *do* this to me, Moss.'

'I'm not *doing* anything.'

'You know what day it is. Come on. It's time.' He stood over Moss, his bear-like frame blocking the light.

What choice did she have? She dragged herself to her feet and followed him down the winding staircase, all the way to the ground. The basket was waiting for her at the foot of the steps.

'Take it and get behind me.' Pa thrust the basket into her arms and picked up his axe.

A blast of trumpets screeched from the high walls. Everyone stopped what they were doing. The Armoury door yawned wide; two hundred soldiers poured out and marched across the courtyard to the gates.

Pa pulled the black hood over his face. Moss knew what was coming. All around them, people shrank back. Some shuddered, some crossed themselves. Some turned their heads as though a foul stench pricked their noses. Moss could have cried with shame. But what good would that do? So she stared at her boots, trying to shut out the whispers.

Stay back . . . The Executioner . . . the basket girl . . . don't go near them. They touch death.

'Come on,' said Pa and yanked her into the march of the procession.

Over the walls of the Lion Tower came the howl of animals in the Beast House. Moss had never seen the beasts, but their roars echoed over Tower Green every time the bell was rung, or the cannons fired, or on a day like today when the shouts from the hill stirred them in their cages.

The procession marched on. Over the narrow moatbridge to the great gate. Once more the fanfare blasted from the turrets and the portcullis was raised. Moss was knocked back by the roar of the crowd. She dropped her basket, covering her ears.

'Pick it up,' said Pa. His voice was flat.

'Pa, all these people . . . there must be twice as many as last time.'

'Just walk.'

She walked, following the slow line of soldiers up the muddy path of Tower Hill. All around her the crowd heaved and pushed, and those that weren't complaining cried out their business.

'Carvings, carvings. Last true likeness of a condemned man!'

'Tragic Tom on a tankard! A little piece of history to take home!'

'Ladies and gents! The Ballad of Poor Sir Tom! Cry like a baby or yer money back!'

Moss hurried on beside Pa. They were nearly at

the top of the hill. And though the crowd pressed her from all sides, she caught a glimpse of the sprawling city beyond. It was smoke and shadows, dark as a cellar. A mystery. A place she would never go. Her world was the Tower. And the only time she set foot outside its walls was the slow walk to the scaffold on Execution Days.

She glanced across at Pa. His hooded head was bowed, just like always. His axe held respectfully by his side, just like always. And, just like always, it made Moss cringe.

'Out of the way, you wretches!' Soldiers were shoving the front row, who shoved viciously back. 'Make way for the Lord Lieutenant of the Tower!'

Lieutenant William Kingston. Doublet drawn tight round his girdled waist, chest puffed, savouring every step of his slow walk up the hill. He was a man with an eye to a title. That's what people said. In the space of a month, he had organised the executions of three monks and a bishop. It seemed to Moss as though the whole of London flocked to the hill. To see the monks dragged to Tyburn. To see Bishop Fisher's head roll. And today the beheading of the man who was once the King's best friend. Sir Thomas More. No wonder people were calling it 'the Bloody Summer'.

She felt the crowd surge forward and she struggled to stay in line while the soldiers pushed them back. The Lieutenant bowed low. His guests had arrived, sweeping towards the bank of seats by the scaffold. There was the tight-lipped man who came to every execution. Next to him another man, straight-nosed, eyes like stones. In front of them both was a lady, her face hidden, shrouded in a cloak of deep blue velvet. And now whispers were stirring in the crowd.

The Queen . . . Queen Anne Boleyn is watching . . .

Anne Boleyn. The Firecracker Queen. She'd come from nowhere. Dazzled the King and blown a country apart. People didn't like her, Moss knew that. She'd stayed in the Tower once. The night before her coronation. And though Moss hadn't seen the Queen herself, she'd heard plenty of tongues clacking. They said that her clothes were too showy. Her manners too French. That she was an upstart who didn't know her place.

Moss took a good look. Was that *really* her? The velvet cloak, too heavy for summer, weighed down her small frame. She didn't look much like a firecracker, thought Moss. More like a broken twig. Her movements seemed fragile. Hiding under the shadow of her cloak, her face was anxious. And when the stone-eyed man said something in her ear, she flinched.

Now the drum was beating. The Yeomen were coming. Forcing their way up the path to the hill, bright in their red and yellow livery.

Moss peered round Pa to get a better look. The Yeomen were bunched in a tight wall around the prisoner, but there he was. Slow as an old bull in the July heat. Sir Thomas More was a good man, people said. A devout man. But King Henry the Eighth had no time for goodness or devotion if it didn't get him what he wanted. And Moss wondered at how quickly the King's best friend could become his bitterest enemy, with all of London jostling for a glimpse of his death.

In the Tower the bell began to toll. Moss clutched her basket.

It was time.

All around her the crowd was pressing.

On the scaffold Pa was waiting.

Sir Thomas climbed the steps, his white cotton gown laced loosely about his neck. White so the blood would show. And at that moment, Moss wished so desperately that Pa would lay down his axe. Punch a soldier. Leap off the scaffold, grab her and dive into the crowd. Let them take their chances in one glorious dash for freedom.

She drilled her gaze at Pa.

He wasn't going anywhere. That was obvious.

She saw his eyes flicker through the slits in his hood and there was a cheer as he took out the blindfold. She watched Sir Thomas push a pouch of coins into his hands. It was the custom of course, but she hated that Pa took it. Money for a good death. Make it quick. Make it painless. Pay and pray.

She fixed her eyes on the straw. Spread in a wide arc around the block, it would soon be soaking in wine-dark blood. Behind her the crowd hushed, looking on hungrily as Sir Thomas let Pa guide his neck into position.

The hill held its breath.

Pa raised his axe.

With a single blow, it hit the block. Clean. Just like always.

The crowd exhaled. From inside the Tower a cannon fired and a cloud of white doves fluttered over the turrets, their heads dyed red. Everyone gasped. It was all Moss could do to stop herself throwing up.

On the scaffold Pa stood over the slumped body of Sir Thomas, wiping his axe on the sack. That was her cue.

She thumped the basket on the ground. The Lieutenant plucked Sir Thomas's dripping head from the straw and lobbed it over the edge of the scaffold, where it landed with a whack in the basket. The crowd went wild.

Moss picked up the basket. Pa was by her side now. She couldn't look at him. Instead she concentrated on getting down the hill without stumbling. She was glad of the distraction and tried not to notice Sir Thomas's unmoving eyes, rolled forever to the sky.

CHAPTER TWO
The Prisoner

'I'm not touching that thing, so don't even bother to ask!'

'Leave the axe then, just help me with the broadswords –'

But Moss wasn't listening. She clomped out of the forge, slammed the door and kicked the water bucket hard, sending a spray of drops into the bitter morning air. It was freezing. Even for January. Fog every night, frost every morning, with a chill that Moss couldn't shake from her bones.

Six months had passed since the beheading of Sir Thomas. A bloody summer, a miserable autumn and a long, cold winter that wasn't over yet.

It was barely dawn, but already the people of the Tower were up and busy. Stable lads were trundling oat barrels over the courtyard and kitchen girls bickered as they carried breakfast to the Lieutenant's Lodgings. From the open shutter behind her came the rasp of bellows, breathing life into the fire. When he wasn't chopping heads on the hill, Pa worked as Tower blacksmith. The little stone forge where they lived was set apart from the bigger buildings of the Tower. Huddled against the East Wall like a cornered mouse, it had been Moss's home for as long as she could remember.

'Moss! Come inside! Now!'

She shivered. A fog was rolling in from the river, curling over the high walls, fingers poking through the cold stone turrets. Tower folk crossed themselves when the river fog came. It was a silent creeper. A hider. A veil for the unseen things.

Things that might crawl from the water. From the black moat, or from the swirling river that slipped and slid its way through London, treacherous as a snake. But whatever it was that made them afraid, it had never shown itself to Moss. The fog didn't scare her.

'Moss!'

She gave the bucket another kick.

'Will you come in?'

She sighed and dragged herself back through the forge door. Inside, Pa was polishing the axe.

'Bread and cheese for you on the table.'

'I'm not hungry.'

Pa turned the axe, rubbing oil into the blade. It was his little ritual and he did it every morning.

'When there's food on the table, you should eat.'

Moss said nothing. What was there to say? This was her life and she just had to accept it. Pa was the Tower Executioner. She was his helper. They were prisoners and *this* was pretty much *it*, because they were never getting out. She'd asked Pa a thousand times how they'd ended up in the Tower. Each time she got the same gruff reply. Pa had been a blacksmith. And then a soldier. Accused of killing a man in his regiment, he and Ma had gone on the run. They'd hidden in a river, where the shock of the icy water sent Ma into labour.

'If I hadn't seen it with my own eyes, I would never have believed it,' Pa had said. 'It was a miracle. You swam from your mother until your fingers broke the surface. Then you held on to me with those fierce little fists. And I didn't let go.'

Of course, the soldiers got Pa in the end. And he would have been executed there and then had it not been for his captain. Pa was the captain's finest swordsman. His kills were clean and accurate. And rather than waste such a talent, the captain wanted to put it to good use. For he was William Kingston, the new Lieutenant of the Tower of London. And he wanted Pa to be his Executioner.

That was all Pa would say. Every time Moss begged him to tell her more, he clammed up. 'Your mother died on the day you were born. We're prisoners now. End of story.'

But *how* could it be the end, thought Moss? Out there was a river and a city. Beyond that were fields. And beyond the fields were places she could only dream about. Places she would go one day.

She stared at Pa, and coiled the end of one of her tangle-curls round her finger. *Rub rub.* His knuckles were white, working the axe blade to a blinding shine. There was less than a week to go until he'd use that axe again. Moss felt her stomach sink to her boots. She wished she were anywhere but here.

'Armourer's keeping us busy today,' said Pa. 'Longswords and broadswords. Two boxes. Rusted and broken. Need to get that fire really hot. More wood from the pile . . .' He stopped. There was a boy standing in the doorway. Moss had seen him before. He worked in the kitchens.

'What do you want?' said Pa gruffly.

'Cook says she's short-handed. Needs an extra

body to fetch and carry fer the prisoners. Says to bring the basket girl.'

Pa hesitated. 'We're busy in here today.'

The boy cocked his head to one side. 'You ever seen Mrs Peak angry? Got a temper hot as a bunch of burnin faggots. If *she* says bring the basket girl, *that's* what I'm doin.'

'Well, it's not a good time –'

'Forget it, Pa, I'm going,' said Moss. Anything was better than being stuck in the forge with a father who chopped off heads. She was out of the door before he could stop her.

'Frost is here! Ice is coming! And devil knows what crawling from the river! Close that door, you little scrag-end!'

Moss was quick enough to duck the blow from Mrs Peak's fist.

'Well, what are you waiting for? Christmas? Take this soup up to the Abbot and be quick about it or

I'll cut off yer ears and boil them for stock!'

Moss looked around eagerly. She'd never set foot in the kitchen before. Never spoken to a cook or a spit boy. Never carried a meal across the courtyard. But this was a chance, wasn't it? To be one of them? A kitchen girl. Not a basket girl.

A bowl of steaming broth stood on a table near the fireplace. She reached for it and felt a sudden sting on her cheek.

'Ow!'

A dob of hot apple dropped to the floor. On the other side of the table a kitchen girl licked her fingers, shooting Moss a scornful glance while another one sniggered behind her apron.

Moss wiped her burning cheek and turned away from the girls. Maybe fitting in wasn't going to be so easy. She picked up the bowl of soup, then ducked as the lumpen fist of the Cook swung over her head once more. It clipped the spit boy in a puff of flour.

'What was that for?' he wailed, dropping his pail of water.

Mrs Peak clouted him again. 'One for the basket girl and another for all this mess!' The tide of water from the spit boy's pail slopped against the table legs, sending the kitchen girls into a spasm of giggles.

'Hell's bells!' bellowed Mrs Peak. 'I'm surrounded by idiots! Lazy girls and halfwit boys! I'd get more help from a bag of mice!'

Moss walked slowly to the kitchen door, balancing the bowl as carefully as she could. She felt another hot slap on her shoulder.

Basket girl. Bloodstained girl. Filthy little basket girl.

Basket girl, when you're dead, who will carry all the heads?

The chants of the girls rang after her down the corridor. She felt a sob rise from her chest and swallowed it back down. She would not cry.

It wasn't easy carrying a bowl of soup, slip-sliding across Tower Green. In winter, the looming walls shut out every sliver of sunlight, turning the grass to mud. Her fingers clutched the warm bowl. There was a little less soup in it now and she hoped the Abbot would not be angry.

Moss had seen them bring the Abbot in a boat from the river through Traitors' Gate, two months back. He'd wobbled when the soldiers hauled him to his feet. Maybe he'd never been in a boat before, thought Moss. Or maybe he was afraid. Behind him, the barred gate swung shut, jaws closing. The black water of the moat flickered with burning torches. Few who came through Traitors' Gate ever made it back out. The Tower was a place of death.

Moss stood outside the Lieutenant's Lodgings. In front of her two guards blocked her path, halberds crossed. This was the only way in to the Bell Tower. They'd put the Abbot right at the top in Sir Thomas's old cell.

She hesitated. 'Soup for the Abbot's breakfast?' she said, half expecting them to send her straight back to the forge with a clipped ear. But they let her pass. A wood-panelled corridor gave way to a narrow stone arch and a set of stone steps. Moss climbed, twisting up and up to a half-landing where another guard stood outside an oak door.

'Soup for the Abbot?' said Moss.

The guard unlocked the door. Moss gripped the bowl and stepped in.

The Abbot was on his knees, mumbling a prayer. In front of him was an empty fireplace. Wood had been scarce this winter and unless a prisoner could pay, his hearth stayed cold.

'Frost is upon us,' said the Abbot, without turning. 'Frost, then ice. A real winter. Cold as the coldest I have known.'

He lifted his head. Straggling hair framed his face and his shaved crown sprouted wild tufts. Two months in a cell didn't always turn you into a crazy man, but it made you *look* like one, thought Moss.

Moss offered the bowl and the Abbot motioned to a small table.

'Soup?' he said.

'Yes,' said Moss, 'I . . . I carried it as best I could. But the mud and . . . I spilt some. I'm sorry.'

The Abbot wrinkled his eyes at Moss. 'Yes,' he said. 'I do believe you are.'

He creaked off his knees and hobbled to a chair by the table. Moss hovered by the door, unsure whether to go or wait for him to finish. The Abbot slurped the soup, his lips trembling a little each time he raised the wooden spoon to his mouth.

'Well, I'll say this,' he said. 'Even lukewarm, this is tasty soup. Better than I'd be getting back in the Abbey.' He slurped some more. 'And I'm used to silence of course. A cold room, a hard pallet; all part of a monk's life. There's one thing I do miss though.' He put down the spoon, picked up the bowl and put it to his lips, draining the last of the soup. 'Would you like to know what?'

Moss nodded shyly.

'My morning walk through the wood. Startled deer. Beech leaves underfoot. And the flute-song of the mistle thrush, calling from the treetops.'

He handed her the bowl. 'What's your name, kitchen girl?'

'It's Moss, Abbot.'

'Then thank you, Moss. It was good soup.'

Moss took it and trod slowly back down the Bell Tower stairs. She tried to picture the Abbot walking among trees with the song of birds above. She would give anything to walk in such a wood.

CHAPTER THREE
The Song of the River

There'd been a strangeness about Pa these past days. A tetchiness that began each time she was about to leave for the kitchen.

'Don't talk to those kitchen girls. They're trouble.'

'You don't have to tell me, Pa.'

'Just keep yourself to yourself. We don't mix with Tower folk. It's best that way.'

'Best for who?' muttered Moss as she stomped across the courtyard. Had he even *tried* to get to know anyone here? Did he not *mind* being treated like a shovelful of scrapings from the garderobe? To the people of the Tower, she and Pa were a bad smell, to be avoided like the plague.

And yet the Abbot didn't think so, did he? Moss had been taking his meal every morning and evening, and while she waited for his bowl, he talked to her. *Talked.* He didn't turn away, or call her names, or flick apple, or try to trip her. And for those few precious minutes, Moss felt like an ordinary girl. Of course, she hadn't told him about her basket. Or about Pa, who'd soon be standing over him, axe raised. But that was the point. It wasn't her. It wasn't Pa. It was what they *did* that made them so repellent to the people of the Tower.

She pushed at the kitchen door. Inside, the room steamed and bubbled with the usual ferocious mix of boiling pans and shrieks from the Cook.

'Mutton pie on the table!' yelled Mrs Peak as soon as Moss walked in. 'No nibbling! No licking! Or it'll be tongue pie tomorrow!'

Moss grabbed the pie and was out of the kitchen with only a jab in the ribs as she darted round the kitchen girls.

It was dusk and the Green was quiet. Without a breath of wind to wheeze through the turrets, Moss could hear the creak of ships and the shouts of the watermen on the river. It was a rare sound. Like music, thought Moss. Notes from the world outside, fluttering into her cold stone box.

She didn't see him coming until it was too late.

Before she knew what was happening, her legs were whipped from under her and Moss found herself falling backwards into the horse trough. Struggling to sit up, she peeled the wet hair from her eyes and scowled at the face leering down at her.

George 'Two-Bellies' Kingston. A squat version of his uncle, red-faced, with a stomach full enough to burst his jacket. With time on his hands, he roamed the Tower, picking on anyone he thought he could bully. He wasn't fussy. Moss kept out of his way as much as she could.

'What's the matter, basket girl? Never had a bath?'

Before she could react, he grabbed her dress with his thick fists and plunged her head under. Suddenly she was gulping filthy water, spluttering as he yanked her head back out. Two-Bellies grinned at her, drunk as a tick on the sight of Moss rasping lungfuls of air.

'Scum always floats to the surface,' he said.

'And pigs can't help that they stink so bad.'

His ham fists forced her under again and this time when she came up, she spluttered, 'Get your hands off me, meat boy.'

'But *that*,' sneered Two-Bellies, 'wouldn't be nearly so much fun, would it, forge rat?' He gave her a last shove and stepped back, shaking his wet sleeves.

Moss heaved herself from the trough. She was soaking from her head to her waist.

The pie! Where was it?

'Looking for this?' Two-Bellies kicked the pie out from under the trough. It lay on the cobbles by his feet, broken in two. Two-Bellies tipped it with the toe of his calfskin boot. 'Rat pie? For your supper?'

'No,' said Moss. 'Mutton pie. For the Abbot.'

'Pigswill pie. For a traitor.'

'What do *you* know, Two-Bellies?'

'I know this.' He raised his boot and brought his foot down hard, crushing the pie into the cobbles. 'In a week's time, that stinking Abbot will be crow-food.'

He wiped his boot on Moss's dress and walked away.

Moss knelt on the cobbles. She daren't go back to the kitchen. All she could do was scrape what was left of the pie back on to the plate.

In the Bell Tower, the Abbot was on his knees, praying as usual. At least the guards had lit a fire tonight to keep him warm. Moss set the pie on the small table. The Abbot took his seat.

'They gave you mutton pie tonight, Abbot, not broth. Only . . . there was an accident on the way.'

The Abbot raised his eyebrows at the state of

his supper, but noticing Moss was dripping wet, he beckoned her towards the fire.

'Pie is pie,' he said. 'Whole, halved or crushed, it is still pie. A man is grateful for pie in his last few days. Even that fearsome Cook has a merciful streak.'

He picked a chunk from the plate and offered it to Moss.

'Here. Take this back for your supper.'

Moss shook her head.

'No, thank you.' Bitterness rose in her gullet. She swallowed it down.

'Well, I may be a dead man, but I know a good meal when I smell one.' The Abbot bit into a piece of pie.

'Abbot . . .'

'Yes?'

'Do you think about *it*?'

'You mean my fast-approaching execution? Well, there's a serious question from one so young.'

He folded his hands into the loose sleeves of his

robe. 'When I was your age, I had no thought of death at all. It was too far away. But I will be honest with you, Moss. Now I do find myself wondering how I will be when the moment comes. Will I be steady? Will I cry out? Will I bow my head and give way to my fate with dignity?'

He munched, flecks of pastry bobbing on his beard. 'But tonight I have a pie. I will think on that. And on the skilled hands of the Cook who made it. And *you*.' He turned to Moss. '*You* are too young to dwell on morbid thoughts. None of us can foretell our end.'

He smiled at her and Moss felt sick. This time next week, his head would be in her basket.

The forge door was shut tight. Moss heaved it open, spilling the glow from the fire over the frozen cobbles. Inside, Pa was putting away his hammer and tongs. He barely looked up.

With her back to him, she sat on the small stool

by the fire and let her gaze drift into the gleam of the red-hot embers.

'Moss?'

'Don't talk to me.'

She stared into the fire, trying not to think about what was coming. About how her father would execute the Abbot. A man who shared his supper. Who'd been nothing but kind. Next week Pa would do his job. And he'd do it without so much as a blink.

'Time you were in bed, Moss. There's fog rolling in from the river.'

'So?'

'Take the extra blanket.'

Moss snorted and climbed on to her pallet. But she didn't protest when he unfolded the blanket and tucked it tightly round her.

A whistle of wind buffeted the window, blowing wisps of clammy fog into the forge. Pa glared at the gap between the shutters. Both of them jumped as the door banged open. Moss's nose wrinkled at the familiar smell of ale and old wee.

'Dear friends, on a night as cold as this, have you a drop of ale to warm an old lady's throat?'

'No we haven't,' growled Pa.

'Come and warm yourself by the fire, Nell,' said Moss, and was off her pallet before Pa could stop her. 'We've bread. And cheese.' She took the cheese from the table and pressed it into Nell's hands. 'You'll like it, it's good and soft.'

Nell's cloudy eyes crinkled. 'Thank you, child. Makes a nice change from rats.'

Moss led her to a chair, feeling Pa's frown on her back.

Nell was old. So old that no one could quite remember what she was doing in the Tower in the first place. She slept in a cellar under the kitchen and caught more rats than any of the cats. It was true that she smelt like a 200-year-old ham. And fair enough, any chair she sat on was always a little damp when she got up. But Moss had never really understood Pa's objection to Nell. During her long life, Nell had lived both inside and outside the

Tower. She knew the Tower's stories and its legends. Secret passageways and walking ghosts and creatures from the deep river and tales of the wide world that lay beyond. And when Nell spoke about chalky hillsides or blue-flowered woods, it was the closest thing Moss had to seeing those things for herself.

'You don't mind if I loosens me rags?' said Nell.

'Course not,' said Moss. 'Just make yourself comfortable.'

Nell bent over and peeled the rags from her misshapen feet. She waggled them in front of the fire and soon a rancid steam was rising from her toes.

'How about a story, Nell?' said Moss. 'The Two Princes! *Please*, Nell.'

Nell chuckled. 'I must have told that story to you a thousand times, child.'

'Then tell it again. Please.'

Nell turned to Pa. 'Child went missing from the river last night, Samuel.'

Pa grunted. 'The river's a dangerous place. Children drown all the time.'

'This wasn't no drowning. Frost is here and the fishermen are saying –'

'I don't care what the fishermen are saying! Superstitious nonsense. And I won't have talk of it in my forge.'

Nell sucked on her cheese. The shutters rattled, drawing little puffs of mist into the room.

'Gaps need plugging,' said Pa. 'I'm off to the stables to get some hay. Make sure that door stays shut now.'

Moss rolled her eyes.

When Pa had gone, Moss grabbed his ale jug from the table and thrust it into Nell's hands.

'Here, Nell. There's a little in there, I think.'

'Such kindness for an old leftover like me.'

Moss settled on the floor by Nell's chair and drew her knees tight to her chest.

'What did the fishermen see, Nell? On the river last night?'

The old lady patted Moss's head.

'Many are the children who have strayed from the shore, who've felt cold fingers of ice close round their ankles. Whose screams are lost in the roar of the river.'

'They fall into the river and drown?'

'Drown, yes. Fall, no. They are *taken*.'

'Taken?'

Nell spat on her hand and crossed herself quickly. 'By the Riverwitch.'

Moss felt a shiver lick her spine. 'The Riverwitch . . .'

'Yes, child. The Witch of the Rivers. She is not always there, but those children she finds in her waters she will take.'

'I'm not afraid of the river, Nell.'

'Is that right?' Nell's cloudy eyes became suddenly sharp. 'Well, perhaps you should be, girl.'

'Have *you* ever seen her? The Riverwitch?'

'I have not and thankful for it.'

'Then they're just stories.'

'Stories. Memories. Who's to say what's true and what's not? My grandmother, rest her rotten bones, told me tales of the river that would scare the skin off an apple.'

'Tell me one now then,' said Moss. Maybe they were just stories, but she loved to hear them. 'Please, Nell. Tell me about the Riverwitch.'

Nell glanced at the door.

'Please, Nell, *please*.'

The old lady lowered her voice. 'Very well. But this story is a sad one and has no end.' She took a swig from the jug and leant forward, seeming glad of her audience in a warm forge on a damp night.

'Long ago, on a bend of this very river, there was a mill, built where the water flows fast. A mill with a crooked chimney and a great wheel of wood that churned the grey river day and night. The Hampton Wheel they called it. Here lived a miller and his daughter. A good girl, who helped her father and who never complained at the work. A fair girl, whose skin was smooth and pale, not like the rugged girls from the fields. A purer soul there never was. All could see the miller's daughter would make some man a fine wife one day.'

Nell paused for a swig.

'Plenty would have wed the girl, sure enough. The goatherd. The weaver's son. But it was another who caught her heart.'

'Who?' said Moss.

'A lordly young soldier with a bright sword and a shine on his tongue. Who passed through one day. Who found bed and board with the miller. Who noticed the miller's daughter. And caught by his charms, the miller's daughter soon fell for the soldier.'

'They were married?'

Nell swilled a mouthful of ale.

'The day was set for their wedding. A wedding feast for the whole village. The miller proud. His daughter's heart so full she thought it might fly away with happiness. They waited. And they waited. And the girl's fingers plucked the cornflowers in her bridal posy. But her soldier did not come.'

'He didn't come? Where was he?'

'A soldier he was, but high-born, who never would have wed a country girl.'

'So what happened to the miller's daughter, Nell?'

'The girl grieved for her soldier and her grief was deep, for she had never once felt pain or sadness her whole life long. After three weary months, she fell sick. A sickness that came and went each morning and lasted all the winter. But when spring sprouted her new shoots, the girl revived. Fairer than ever, she was. Her cheeks now pink and her body full. And the women in the village tittled and tattled and knew what the girl herself did not.'

'Knew what, Nell?'

'That she was with child.'

'Oh,' said Moss.

'Yes. And sure enough, as the May sun turned green fields to gold, the miller's daughter had her baby. A little boy. And though he was brown-eyed and brown-haired like his father, the miller's daughter loved him and raised him. And nothing was as sweet to her as the feel of her son's embrace.'

'Then this is a happy story, Nell.'

'Not so fast, child. This tale is not yet told. Twelve

years came and went. Until one winter's morning, the wind blew the sound of hooves from the high path to the mill. Men on horseback. The miller's daughter watched them come. Four greys and a fifth, a fierce white horse, carrying a steward.'

'A what?'

'A man who would stop at nothing to do his master's bidding. For his master was none other than the young soldier, now a noble lord, rich from his father's estate, lying on his deathbed, with no child of his own to carry his family name. The lord knew the miller's daughter had given birth to a son. And from the gossip that spread from the village fields to the kitchens of his estate, he knew the son was his.'

Nell shook her head sadly. 'Property of that noble lord was the child. So the steward took the boy, tossed three gold sovereigns to the miller and told them they would never see the child again.

'Now the miller was greedy. Three gold sovereigns would buy a new millstone. *Forget the boy*, he said to

40

his daughter. He paid no heed to her screams or to the pain that hollowed out her heart. That night she lay awake and a bitter seed, planted in her pure soul, began to grow. When the cockerel crowed in the dawn, she rose quietly and climbed the great millwheel –'

'No, oh, Nell!'

'Did I not tell you this tale was an unhappy one?' Nell drained the last of the ale from the jug. 'The miller's daughter stepped on to the turning wheel and for a moment her graceful body soared as her heart had once soared. Then she plunged, her body smashing through the crust of ice, deep into the river.'

'She drowned?' said Moss in a small voice.

'Drowned she was. Dragged and crushed by the pull and suck of the Hampton Wheel. That day the wheel stopped, never to turn again. The mill fell into ruin. The miller died a poor and lonely man.'

'Serves him right, Nell.'

'Maybe so. But this tale is still not yet told. The

girl's body was broken. But her bitter soul gave life to her tattered remains. And her empty heart filled with the cold spirit of the river. She became –'

'The Riverwitch?' said Moss eagerly.

'Yes, child, the Riverwitch. A restless spirit to haunt its depths each winter. In summer, she is gone. She swims far away to guard her frozen heart. When winter comes, she returns. In her wake, streams become ice and rivers turn so cold that the unwary ones who fall in may not climb out. And in the cold rivers she searches.'

'For what, Nell?'

'For a child to snatch with fingers of ice.'

Nell leant into the fire and her face crackled with shadows. 'The rivers are hers, not ours. Foolish is the one who forgets the song of the river.'

Nell began to croon softly. A song that Moss had not heard before, its melody lilting and incomplete.

Silver river stained with souls
Take care of its depths, my child

When frost and ice creep from her shores
She'll drag you down, my child

A miller's daughter once she was
Spurned on her wedding day
She seeks the thing she'll never have
A loving child to hold

She is the waves, the current strong
The weed that snags your feet
And if she finds you, better drown
Than feel her cold embrace

'ENOUGH!'

In the doorway stood Pa with an armful of hay, his face taut with anger. 'One more note from you, old lady, and I swear, I'll not open my door to you again!'

Nell pursed her lips. Pa threw the hay on the floor.

'I'll not have you filling my daughter's head with all that rubbish.'

Moss jumped up. 'What else is there to fill it with then? Executions? *You* haven't been locked in a fortress all your life. I'm nearly twelve and I've never seen a wood, or a meadow full of flowers. Or –'

'Or nothing. We have no choice. We keep our heads down and get on with it. This is our home.'

'Our tomb, more like.'

'Well, there's nothing I can do about it.'

Moss opened her mouth to reply, then shut it again. What was the point?

The forge was quiet. Moss glared at Pa. He dropped his gaze and said no more.

The silence was broken by a throat-rattling snore from the fire. Nell had fallen asleep, head against the hearth, a trickle of cheese making its way down her chin.

'Pa,' whispered Moss.

'What?'

'We could find . . . a way out? Don't sigh. Remember Lady Tankerville last summer?'

'One escape. *One*. In a hundred years.'

'I know, I know. But isn't it worth a try?'

Pa shook his head. 'And risk getting caught? Hanged? It may be a half-life in here, but at least it's a life.'

'But –'

'Let it go, Moss. Trust me. There's no way out.'

CHAPTER FOUR
Escape

Moss sat on the cobbles, tying her boots as best she could with a broken lace. She had already done her breakfast duties. Now the white winter sun burned away the frost.

Inside the forge, Pa was up, pumping the bellows.

'Where are you going?' he called through the open door.

'Nowhere.'

'Well, don't be too long. Don't go leaning over any walls – do you hear me?'

'No.'

'And stay away from Traitors' Gate. Those steps are slippery. I don't want you falling into the moat. It's deep when the tide is in. Are you listening?'

'No! I'm NOT listening. Because *you* never listen to *me*. And because you say the same old things, EVERY SINGLE TIME!'

She heard the bellows stop. Pa appeared in the doorway. He looked pale. Or maybe it was just ash from the fire. She glared at him.

'Stay away from people. Stay away from the moat. Stay away from the river. This wretched place is bad enough, but *you* make it worse!' She was gone before he could stop her.

The Green was quiet. Just a stable boy filling the troughs. It was a bright, fogless day. Over the walls drifted the sounds of the river. Gulls screeching. Men calling. The groan of ships.

Moss made up her mind. Just one quick look. Never mind Pa.

She darted through the arch towards Traitors'

Gate and scoped the South Wall. The guard had his back to her and was making his slow march along the battlements towards the Cradle Tower. Perfect.

Moss was soon up the steps and scooting along the battlements. She found her spot and wedged her boot into a hole where the wall had worn away. With a push she launched her head and shoulders. Her heart soared. It was here she had the best view of the great River Thames.

Moss leant out as far as she dared, feeling the freedom of the air above and the river below. For a few moments she was blinded by the water, a plate of dazzling silver that threw the sun back into the sky. Then a forest of sails came into focus and she drank in the sight of the river at work. Three-masted ships and hefty barges ploughed stubbornly upriver. Painted Venetian galleys jostled oars for a place at the quay. And dodging among them like a swarm of flies were the watermen in their flat little boats, ferrying passengers from bank to bank. How many times had Moss wondered how different her life could have been? If she'd been one of the children down there on the wharf, fetching and carrying for the traders. Bet none of *their* baskets had heads in.

Moss squinted at London Bridge in the distance. It was almost a town in itself, piled crazily with buildings from one end to the other. It blocked the passage of the wide river, sucking the water through its arches with a force that would rip a tree from its roots.

A flash of red and yellow on the bridge caught her eye. Yeomen. At the Drawbridge Gate. It didn't take a genius to work out what they were up to. A small crowd was gathering. Sure enough there was a cheer as the head of a traitor was unpicked from its spike and tossed into the river. Moss inhaled the salt air and turned away. The outside world was as cruel as the Tower. But more than anything, she longed to be a part of it.

At the other end of the wall, the guard was about to turn. Quickly, Moss made her way back to the steps and scrambled down, leaping the last few on to the cobbles.

A hand grabbed her by the scruff of her dress.

'Naughty naughty.'

Two-Bellies jerked her round, an unpleasant grin on his face. 'What's a dirty little rat like you doing up on the battlements?'

'Trying to get away from the stink of *you*.'

'Stink, is it? Well, I've got a job that'll shut that mouth of yours. Unless you want me to tell the guard you were walking his wall?'

Moss glared at him.

'Thought not,' sneered Two-Bellies. He dragged her along the cobbled path towards the garderobe drop and shoved her down the steps. 'Toilet needs a clean. Off you go.'

Moss had to give him credit. He was organised enough to throw a bucket and shovel after her.

The smell in the garderobe drop was eye-wateringly bad. A low pit underneath the Lieutentant's Lodgings, it was ten feet from the toilet holes above.

Whatever came hurtling down ended spattered halfway back up the brickwork. Seeing she had no choice, Moss dumped the bucket at one end and began scraping the walls.

Half an hour later, Two-Bellies had grown tired of laughing at Moss and had fallen asleep at the top of the steps. Inside the drop, Moss could hear his snores. She picked up her bucket and tiptoed up the steps. Carefully prising the soft boots from his feet, she tipped a dollop of foul slops into each. She allowed herself a smile. It was the little things that made life worth living.

There was no point hanging around until Two-Bellies woke up. Leaving the filthy bucket on the steps, she went back down to get the shovel. As she picked it up, she slipped on the slimy floor, sending the shovel clanging against the wall. She winced, waiting for the echo to stop. But as she stooped to pick up the shovel again, she noticed a fist-sized gap in the wall where it had knocked out a brick.

Moss squatted down. A draught hissed across her

cheek and she put her hands to the gap, plugging the sharp breath of wind. That was strange. Where was the wind coming from? She leant on one of the large wall stones above the gap and it moved. Curious, she pressed the full weight of her shoulder against it. Without too much resistance, the stone swivelled and she found herself peering into blackness.

Moss wriggled her head and shoulders through the hole. She was looking into some sort of enclosed space. Gradually, her eyes got used to the dark and she could see it was a small chamber, lined with rough stone. Where the floor should have been was the gaping dark of what looked like a very steep drop.

What was this place? She peered down. Just darkness. A well perhaps?

She turned back to the garderobe drop. Then looked back at the chamber. What harm would it do just to take a peep? Quickly she picked up the shovel and carried it outside. Two-Bellies was still snoring at the top of the steps. She placed the shovel next to the bucket. He would wake and think she'd scarpered.

Guided by the draught, Moss groped her way to the hole and eased herself through, clinging to the stonework, feet scrabbling for a foothold.

One. Two. Her feet found gaps, just big enough for a boot. *Three. Four.* Her hands followed. Down she went. Slowly. Deeper and deeper. The walls around her pressed in, echoing with the scrape of her boots. The air was cold, getting colder with every step. And the walls were wet. Slimed with green, like the riverweed that clung to the stone steps at Traitors' Gate. How far down was she now? Maybe twenty steps? Wherever she was, she must be deep in the foundations of the Tower. At least she wouldn't get lost. The only way was down. Or up.

Her boot squelched into mud and she supposed this must be the bottom. She planted both her feet in the mud carefully, making sure she was on solid ground before letting go of the wall. Funny, it didn't seem so dark here.

She turned. Ahead of her, specks of light pricked

the blackness. She squinted at the light. The specks seemed to be coming from the end of a long, dark passage. What *was* this place? Somewhere so old and forgotten that it could have come from one of Nell's stories.

Now what? Go back? Tell Pa? Or go on? By herself.

She peered down the passage into the darkness. Her heart clanged against her chest.

From somewhere came a sound. Far away. Like the soft rattle of leaves at the top of a tree. It tugged at something deep inside Moss. She pressed her hand to her chest. Her heart was still hammering. But the noise was pulling her.

She bent her head and stepped forward.

CHAPTER FIVE
River Thief

The roof of the passage was low. Several times she banged her head. Mud and water sloshed round her boots. The light was distant and grey, but it was enough to follow. Moss ran her fingers over the walls. They were earth and rock. She hardly noticed the flints in the mud as they nicked her thin-soled boots. The noise was louder now and there was a rhythm to it. Like breathing. It mixed with the short gasps that stuck in her throat. Excitement. Fear. She didn't know what. All she could think about was getting to the end of the passage. The further she went, the brighter the specks of light became.

Moss stopped, feeling rock ahead of her. She looked up. There was a shaft of brightness coming from above. She scrambled up towards it and gripped the rough walls, pulling herself on to a ledge a few feet above the base of the tunnel. In front of her was a hole blocked with large stones, grey light filtering through.

Carefully, Moss dislodged the stones. She stuck her head out of the hole and almost tumbled backwards. Above her were the creaking planks of a wharf. And through the murky half-light was a band of shimmering silver, spreading as far as she could see.

It was the river. She could hardly believe it. She was outside the Tower. She was . . . free.

Her heart was beating so fast she thought it might burst from her chest. The passage was *a tunnel*? A tunnel from the garderobe drop all the way under the moat to the riverbank.

Moss was shaking now, her ears pounding with blood and crazy, mixed-up thoughts. For years she'd listened to Nell's tales. Of ghosts and witches and old passageways and siege tunnels dug by fearful kings. And she'd never known whether to believe the tales or not. Of course, Pa had scorned them. They were just stories dribbled from an old lady's lips. But this tunnel was real. As real as the mud beneath her feet.

She was free.

On her lips, the tang of salt and riverweed. The sweetest thing she'd ever tasted.

Moss looked around. She could wade out from under the wharf and, if the water wasn't too deep, make it along the wharf's edge to the bank. She could see that the tunnel would probably be flooded at high tide, which would account for all the water and mud. She reckoned she had an hour, maybe two, before it flooded again. Her head was bursting and all the while she felt a *tug-tug*, deep inside, drawing her to the river. She had never been this close to it.

Before she was even aware of what she was doing, Moss had hitched up her dress, crawled through the hole and dropped into the water.

It wasn't very deep at all. She waded swiftly, enjoying the tingle of icy water as it rinsed round her boots. With a few strides she was out from under the wharf. The water was deeper here, up to her thighs. Beyond the wharf, she could see waves lashing the shingle bank, peeling back in a snarl of froth. The wind was picking up and she felt the pull of the current now, tearing at her legs. Her boots were slipping on the shingle bed. She stumbled and steadied herself. The current was strong.

She carried on wading, the murky water driving against her body. She staggered as her foot struck something large. And at that same moment, her legs were whipped from under her and she stumbled sideways, flailing into the deeper water of the river.

Instantly a fist of current snatched her under.

She felt her body barrel under the waves, over

and over, cracking her head on something hard. She tried to open her eyes, but all she could see was a wall of dark. Panicking for breath, she gulped and felt saltwater fill her lungs, while useless legs thrashed against the flow that towed her as easily as a piece of rope. Her head was numb in the freezing river. She was seeing things now. Dizzy, flickering pictures, of Pa raising his axe, Two-Bellies leering at her, the swirling crowd on the hill. Then the images sank away, deep down into the silt, and Moss was bursting, her chest a choked balloon of salty water. Which way was up? Which was down? Both were gone, dissolved in the hideous pull that sucked her into darkness. That was when she saw the face.

A woman. Her hair wispy and coiling, like smoke. A pale, frozen face, lit by strange eyes, with no expression, no smile or frown. Around her, seaweed fanned out. Her bare arms reached up towards Moss. A poor drowned soul, lost to the river. And Moss knew, sure as rotten teeth on a rich man, that she would soon be joining her. The suck of the current stopped. She felt her dress billow as her feet tipped upwards.

Without warning, there was a sudden jerking at her legs. She felt the dead weight of her body being dragged from above. Beneath her, the woman shrank backwards into the black river.

Feet first, Moss felt herself hauled through the waves until her head broke the surface in a splutter of foam. Arms were pulling her now, dragging her body until it cracked on the side of something solid. More heaving and she flopped on to her back against wooden planks, her lips spitting frothy vomit. Then the grey sky went white.

'Sweet Harry's scabs! That's a wind cold enough to freeze off yer goosters.'

Words were buffeting Moss's ears. Fuzzy at first. Then gradually more distinct as she came to her senses.

'Take a punt up to Old Swan . . . no time for anything else now.'

From under the wisps of her lashes, Moss peeked out. A blurry shape was moving around her.

'Ain't nothin here worth havin.'

She felt hands patting her dress.

'Stupid pisspot of a shore girl.'

She kept her eyes closed, peeping through her lashes until the blurry shape grew a face. Brown-eyed and smudged with dirt. Hands, going through her pockets. Scrawny arms and shoulders, clothed in a threadbare tunic. Hair dark and matted, as though a cat had chewed it up and spat it out.

It was a boy. And judging by the way he was cussing, he seemed very cross.

'Should have known yer'd be good fer nothin but a boatful of sick.'

Slowly, Moss opened her eyes. The boy did not notice at first, but carried on sifting through her pockets. She blinked, then heaved herself up on one elbow and felt the ground wobble.

'Stay on yer back, yer nubbin loach!' He shot her a furious glance.

Still groggy, Moss looked around and saw she was sitting in a small flat boat, bobbing near the shore. A boat! On the river! How had she . . . how did she . . .?

'Sweet Harry's gammy leg! I said stay *still*!' The boy gave her a push.

'Ow!'

'Idiot shore girl! You'll have me boat over!'

He glared at her. She glared back.

'All right,' she said. 'I'll keep still.' She looked about. The boat was a good way from the shore. 'Could you tell me . . . what happened?'

'You fell in the river, I pulled you out, you puked in me boat.'

'Oh.'

The boy said nothing. He had his back to her now and was checking a net trailing in the water behind him.

'Is this your own boat?'

The boy ignored her, still sifting through his net.

'It must be nice to have a boat.'

Silence.

'I mean, nice to be able to come out here. On the river.' She was running out of things to say.

'What are you talkin about, *nice*? I rows to make me livin. Ain't nothin nice about rowin the river.'

'I just meant, you know, in your boat you can go wherever you like, see all the other boats, the sails, everything –'

'What? Are you mad as a rabbit? It ain't no pageant out here. Them big boats would squash you soon as look at you. Saw a waterman go down only last week. *His* boat was a four-seater. Crushed between a galley an' a barge like a fly between yer thumbs.'

'Oh. I didn't know.'

'Well, you do now.'

The boy took up his oars and began to row towards the bank. Moss watched, surprised his scrawny arms could pull such deft, clean strokes.

His clothes were little more than rags, and she saw that his tunic had been patched many times and that the patches were sackcloth. He really was filthy. She wondered at how a boy who worked on the river could *be* so dirty. Every bit of skin was grimed, as though he hadn't been within two miles of a pail of water his whole life.

'So . . . what's your name?' said Moss.

'What you want that for?'

'Well, to thank you, I suppose. You just saved my life?'

'Fat lot of good that's done me.'

'Well, I didn't *ask* you to save me. Look, I'm sorry I was sick in your boat . . . My name's Moss.'

'Sounds about right. Useless green stuff, soaks up water.'

A gust of wind rocked the little boat, biting into Moss's body. Her woollen dress was sodden and grey water was pooling where she sat. Her teeth were rattling and before long, her legs and arms were shaking too.

'Do you . . . do you . . . have . . . a blanket?'

'You what? A *blanket*? Who do you think I am? Some lordy merchant sailin a ship piled high with furs an' silky pillows?'

'It's c-cold.'

'So? Shouldn't have gone swimmin then, should yer?'

'I didn't go swimming. I was walking. I fell –' She gripped her feet with her frozen fingers. They were bare. 'Where are my boots?'

'What?'

'My boots. I was wearing boots when I fell in.'

'Don't ask me. Probably at the bottom of the river stinkin out the fish, in't they?'

The boy was on his feet now, punting the boat towards the bank with one oar. On the shore was a jumble of flimsy huts. Shacks made of driftwood and crates, propping each other up in the mud. They seemed so close to the water, thought Moss. Surely one rogue tide and they'd all be swept away?

'Is this where you live?' she said.

'Who wants to know? Whoever it is, I ain't tellin.' The boy scowled. 'Well, don't just sit there like a nun givin thanks for her own farts. Hop off now, shore girl.' He held the boat fast with the oar and Moss wobbled to the front.

'Won't you tell me your name?'

'Out! Count yerself lucky I didn't tip you back in!'

Moss jumped on to the shingle and the boy pushed off without a backwards glance.

As the little boat nudged into deeper water, he reached over the side and fished out something from the trailing net. Moss squinted at his catch. It didn't look much like fish.

Then she gasped. Her boots! The little thief had stolen her boots!

'Those are mine! Give them back!' she yelled.

But the boy just grinned and carried on rowing up the river.

CHAPTER SIX
Two-Bellies' Revenge

What kind of low life saves your skin then steals your boots?

Alone on the shore, Moss hugged her damp body tight. The ice-wind sliced through her. She had never been so cold. She tried rubbing her arms and legs, but her fingers felt as though they might snap. All she could think about was the fire in Pa's forge. Heat. Warm and dry. She needed to get back home as soon as possible.

Moss looked around. The Tower stood tall against

the grey sky. Good. Not too far off, and at least that little thief had dumped her on the right side of the river. She set off towards the wharf, wincing as her bare feet scraped the stony shore. The ramshackle huts were behind her. On her left, the banks pitched upwards to shadowy streets where dogs barked and people cried out. Down on the shore, it was strangely silent. Just the lap of the incoming tide and the call of boatmen, snatched by the wind. She edged closer to the waterline. Here, the mud was thick and the stones fewer, and though her toes were ready to drop off, Moss savoured the squelch between them. She let the gentle waves wash over her feet.

Crash! Moss found herself thrown backwards. A freak wave threw up a fistful of shingle, whipping her bare ankles. She was on her knees, stumbling to her feet. A noise like laughter tinkled from the water's edge. The shingle rattled, settling back down, raked by the waves. All the same, she retreated from the waterline and hurried as fast as she could back to the wharf. She waded underneath. The water was deeper, much deeper than it had been, and she could see waves sloshing into the tunnel through the gap. She would have to be quick.

Heaving herself up through the hole, Moss dropped back into the tunnel. The water was up to her armpits. She hesitated. Outside she heard the tinkling laughter again. Stop it, she told herself. It's only the river. But as she waded back through the tunnel, her head swirled with the memory of the drowned woman.

'It's just the river,' she said out loud. Her words echoed down the tunnel. 'I'm not afraid.'

Well, perhaps you should be, girl. Somewhere inside her head, Nell's cloudy-eyed warning echoed back. *The rivers are hers, not ours. Foolish is the one who forgets the song of the river.*

It was a tough climb back up to the garderobe drop, frozen fingers slipping, sodden dress dragging every step of the way. By the time Moss reached the garderobe door, the last chimes of the Tower's curfew bell were ringing. She crept up the steps. The yard was empty, so she scurried through the arch to Tower Green, ready to sprint round the White Tower to the forge.

'Hello, basket girl.'

A thick arm swiped her off her feet, then dragged her backwards into the stables, shoving her into the hay. The bulk of Two-Bellies stood over her, his red face redder than usual.

'Think you're so clever? Think you're so funny?'

Moss cast around wildly, wet clothes forgotten. There was only one way out and it was blocked. She glared up at Two-Bellies.

'Let me guess. I ruined your best boots?'

'Don't cheek me, basket scum.'

'What have I got to lose? You're going to beat me up anyway.'

He lunged, but Moss rolled, dodging his swiping fists. She was up on her feet, whip-quick, jumping from the hay.

'You can run but you can't hide, forge rat.'

'Come and get me then.'

Two-Bellies picked up a broom and advanced, blocking any hope of her sprinting to the door. He spread his arms wide, grabbing each end of the broom handle, herding her into the corner.

'Like catching a chicken, see? And when I've got you, I'm going to wring your neck.'

Moss sidestepped another lunge and in the split second of his unbalance, she darted under his waving arm. There was a *whoosh* of air and a crack as the broom made contact with her back. Moss was on her knees. Without a moment's hesitation, Two-Bellies grabbed her neck and shoved her head into a water butt. Now the fists were pushing her down, holding her under until the brown water made her eyes smart.

No breath. The fist was on her neck. Moss felt her chest start to spasm. How many chokes before her lungs filled up? She tried to wriggle from his grip. Her head turned and through the water she saw Two-Bellies' raging face. His fist pressed harder.

Her lungs were exploding. Suddenly she was seized by a paralysing terror. He was actually trying to drown her. After everything that had happened that day . . . finding the tunnel, surviving the wild river, only to be drowned by a meat-faced bully on her own doorstep. And that was the moment when Moss knew what she needed to do. She let herself go limp. The hand on her neck relaxed. Then she struck, jabbing both elbows hard into his chest. Two-Bellies howled and let go, giving Moss time to whip her head out of the water and spring to her feet.

Two-Bellies picked up his broom.

'Come on then! You want some, basket scum?'

Not good. He was still between Moss and the door.

Two-Bellies walked towards her, holding the broom like a quarterstaff.

Definitely not good.

Then instinct took over. It happened so quickly, Moss could barely believe what she'd done. One minute Two-Bellies was yelling and swinging his staff. The next she had stuck out her leg, tripped him over his own weapon and tipped him head first into the water butt. And for a moment, there he lodged, legs waggling.

Sprinting through the door, Moss swept her eyes across the yard. On the far side, Mrs Peak was bawling at a couple of kitchen boys who'd dropped a tray of quails on the cobbles. From the stables came a crash followed by a full-throated roar.

'Nnnaarrgghhhh!'

In a panic, Moss realised Two-Bellies would be out of the stables before she'd had time to run across the Green. She had to hide somewhere, quickly!

She slipped round the corner and through an open door. Inside was a narrow passage and some stairs. She shot up the stairs and along a corridor. She had no idea where she was, but she didn't care. She just had to find somewhere. Anywhere. It didn't matter so long as Two-Bellies couldn't find her.

There were voices coming up the stairs. Moss spotted a door halfway along the corridor, wide open. She poked her head in. The room was empty and silent. All she could hear was the spitting of tallow candles. She darted inside. At one end was a table, spread with a cloth. On the table were dishes piled high with creamy white manchet loaves, their sweet smell mixing with the smoky fat of the burning tallow.

'Lord help us! Have your heads gone to mince?' Mrs Peak's bellow filled the corridor, getting louder as she approached. 'Do you think the Duke likes his quails cold? Put those birds next to that brawn and get a bleedin move on!'

Quick as a cat, Moss dived under the table. There she crouched, stifling her gasping breaths, aware that the stench of the garderobe rose from her like a fog. From behind the cloth, she peeped out and hoped the smoking tallow would mask her stink.

Then Mrs Peak was in the room, flapping her apron at the kitchen boys. 'Be quick with you! The guvnor is coming! The Duke of Norfolk with him!

And when they get here, I daresay they won't want to be gawping at *your* ugly mugs!'

Moss heard the boys fumbling with their dishes. There was a scuffling as they retreated and a 'Thank you, sirs'. Now she heard the *clack-clack* of well-heeled boots entering the room. The door slammed.

CHAPTER SEVEN
The Queen's Uncle

Shivering under the table, Moss gathered her
dress close, trying to stem the trickle of water
at her feet. She curled her body as small as she was
able. She could hear voices.

'No, Lieutenant, it's not going well, damn it! Not
well at all!'

'My Lord Norfolk . . .'

'By Christ and all his wretched saints! There are
days when I think it would be easier to fight a war
than serve the King!'

'Yes, my Lord. Of course, my Lord.'

That was the Lieutenant's voice. Oily words and a bow low enough to make his girdle twang. But the other one. The Duke . . .

She couldn't resist a peek. Carefully, she shuffled forward and tweaked a chink in the cloth. The Lieutenant was still bent double. The Duke loomed over him, his face a brewing storm. He looked . . . familiar.

From her chink, Moss swallowed a little gasp of recognition. It was the stone-eyed man who'd watched Sir Thomas's head roll last summer. The one who'd sat next to Queen Anne Boleyn at the execution. Who'd made her flinch. And judging by the flustered look on the Lieutenant's face, he was here on important business.

'My Lord Norfolk,' said the Lieutenant, 'did you wish to speak with me on some matter?'

'Of course, you fool! I didn't come here to nibble manchets, did I?'

'No, my Lord.'

'As you know, the King has charged me with the task of preparing his Feast Day celebrations at Hampton Court. *I want a St Valentine's Day to remember, Norfolk! And you are the man to make it happen!* Those were His Majesty's words. As if I didn't have enough on my plate.'

'My Lord?'

'The Feast of St Valentine. Lovey-dove dancing. Kissy-kissy couples. All that nonsense. What that court needs is a damn good *fight*! So *that* is what they will get.'

'Yes, my Lord Norfolk.'

'With *your* help, Lieutenant Kingston.'

Moss watched the Lieutenant turn a little pale.

'*My* help, my Lord?'

'Damn right, your help! Those idiots at Whitehall Palace couldn't build a pigsty! Even if you put the hammers right into their hands! I need *your* men. I need soldiers, armourers, your finest horse, the use of your forge.'

'But, my Lord! Pardon the expression, but we

are up to our necks in preparations for the Abbot's execution. In a mere six days –'

'Damn your days!'

The Lieutenant shifted and the rustle of his doublet echoed round the room.

'*You*, Kingston, will make it your personal business to build what I need for the festivities. You will do it in the utmost secrecy. I have drawings. Your men will build to their exact specification. And it will work. If it does not . . . well, I hardly need remind you how changeable is the mood of the King.'

The Lieutenant's throat moved up and down, as if he'd swallowed an egg. The room was quiet. The tallow candles spat.

Moss's bare feet curled on the stone floor, her body quivering in the clench of her sodden dress. She daren't think about what would happen if she were discovered. These were powerful men. Their business was secret. So she stayed as still as she could. At the same time, she couldn't tear herself from the chink in the cloth, fascinated by these men and their talk of masques and palaces and a King who could end a man's life if he chose.

In front of her, the Lieutenant fiddled with the button on his cape.

'Er, permit me, my Lord, to ask after your niece, Anne. Is she in good health?'

Moss's ears pricked. They were talking about the Queen, Anne Boleyn.

The Duke of Norfolk did not reply.

'I have heard –'

'Never mind what you've heard. The Queen is with child. If that child is a boy, all will be well and the King will have a son and heir. If not, then her time is done.'

Moss caught her breath. She should not be here. She should not be listening to any of this. Still she peeked through the cloth. What did he mean, *her time is done?*

'These are sensitive matters, my Lord Norfolk,' said the Lieutenant. 'Difficult times, even for the noblest of families.'

The Duke's eyes narrowed. 'Do you take me

for a fool?'

'No, my Lord?'

'A half-wit perhaps?'

'No –'

'Then put away your idiot presumptions, Kingston,' said the Duke. 'There are many routes to power. All of us have profited from the rise of my niece. Now we wait. We wait and see.'

Their conversation was interrupted by a knock at the door.

'Enter!' barked the Lieutenant.

Moss watched as a breathless man bowed into the room and handed a piece of paper to the Duke.

'Leave us,' said the Duke to the messenger.

He opened the letter. Moss saw his stone eyes turn over its contents. They gave away nothing. It could have been the best news or the worst.

The Duke strode over to the fireplace. He set the end of the letter to the flames, lighting it like a taper.

'I have a man in Whitehall Palace,' he said. 'When a door is closed, he listens for me. He tells me the things I need to know.'

The Duke held up the burning paper. It flared in front of his face and his eyes didn't move. 'The Queen has lost her baby. *She* lives, but the child is dead. And a pity it was not the other way around. For it was a boy.'

Moss caught her breath. In the Duke's hand, the burning letter crumbled to black ash.

'It is over for Anne,' he said. 'Nothing can save her now.'

He strode to the door, leaving the ghosts of his words hanging in the room. All at once, Moss's fear turned to anger. She wanted to leap out from under the table and run after the Duke and shake him and shout at him. The Queen had lost her baby. And what? She might as well be dead? This man, with his eyes of stone and a cold heart – this was a man she would not want for an uncle, not for all the riches in the world.

CHAPTER EIGHT
Keeping a Secret

'What happened to you?'

Pa was hunched over a plate of bread and cheese, frowning at Moss who'd slunk into the forge, wet dress slapping at her ankles.

Moss swallowed. Her head was so full, she barely knew where to begin.

'Well –'

'And *where* are your boots?'

She wanted to blurt out everything to Pa, but she stopped, annoyed by the look on his face. Did he *have* to be so disapproving of everything she did?

'I asked you what happened to your boots.'

'Two-Bellies made me clean the garderobe. I took them off. Someone must have stolen them.'

Half-lies, half-truths. They tripped off her tongue.

'Boots don't come cheap, Moss.'

Moss shrugged. 'I know.'

Pa put down his piece of bread. 'Don't take that tone with me. I worked hard to buy those boots, if you remember? Shod the Armourer's horses then pulled two of his wife's teeth.'

'I can't help it if my boots were stolen.'

'You should take more care. You just aren't careful enough.'

'*Careful?* If you had your way, I'd never set foot out of this forge.'

'That's not true.'

'*Isn't it?*' She stared at him. For a moment his expression changed. A shift in his face. As though there was something he wanted to say. Then it was gone.

'Don't bother,' said Moss. 'Just leave me alone.'

She grabbed a piece of bread and went over to the fire. Her dress was still soaking, so she peeled it off and wrapped herself in a blanket. Then she took the bread and the blanket and curled up on her pallet. The day's events swirled inside her head. She needed time to think.

Pa had finished his supper. She watched him shake the crumbs from his plate into the fire. It was the end of a day like any other. Except it wasn't. *Everything* had changed.

On her lips was the salt tang of the river. She closed her eyes. There it was, sparkling silver in the sunlight. Raking the shingle. The river. She felt it tugging at her legs, bowling her over. Then she shuddered, remembering the empty grasp of the drowned woman, arms reaching towards her. What if that boy hadn't pulled her out? She'd be a drifting corpse by now. Pa would never see her again. She'd never see *Pa* again. Something wrenched inside her. The thought of him, alone.

Moss pulled the blanket tight. But she *hadn't* drowned. What she'd discovered was a way out of this miserable life. A way out of the Tower. And for the first time in a very long while, she felt a little grain of hope.

She hugged herself. She'd never had a secret before. It glowed warm inside her. Her head flickered with the things she'd seen and heard and done that day. Two-Bellies' legs sticking out from the water butt! She'd fought him, beaten him, made him madder than a hornet. Standing up to that meat-faced bully had felt so good.

But the one thing that really stuck in her head was the grin of the smudge-faced river boy. She could see him now. Waving her boots in his scrawny hands. Well, she'd find that boy. Wipe the grin off his face. If she could tip Two-Bellies into a barrel, surely she could handle a thieving river rat?

Moss made up her mind. The very next chance she got, she was going back through the tunnel.

She peeped over her blanket. Pa was by the pail,

washing the day's work from his body. She watched him dry his hands and face with the sackcloth. Eat, work, wash, sleep. Always the same. A rhythm he never broke. Even on Execution Days.

Why *hadn't* she told him about the tunnel?

Something had stopped her. Something about Pa. About the way he couldn't bear to let Moss out of his sight. The way he seemed to fear everything and everyone outside the forge. And now a thought began to scratch away inside Moss's head. A nagging thought that wouldn't go away, no matter how ridiculous it was.

What if he didn't want to leave?

CHAPTER NINE
A Hand in the Darkness

'RAAATTS! RATS IN MY KITCHEN!'

The kitchen door banged open and Mrs Peak erupted into the courtyard, hands on hips, bellowing into the morning.

'Where is she? Five days to execution and the rats are in the flour! Where's that filthy ratcatcher?'

Moss was on her way to the kitchen and caught up with Nell, who was shuffling across the courtyard, trailing her rat sack and the smell of rotting feet.

'Coming, coming,' grumbled Nell. 'Keep your

hose on, you old turnip. What a lot of fuss over a few rats.' She grinned at Moss. 'Come and see me later, child. You can help old Nell skin her catch.'

'All right, Nell.' Moss didn't mind rats. Just as long as she didn't have to eat them.

'About time, you shambling bag of bones!' Mrs Peak raised her mighty fist ready to clout the approaching Nell. 'Now get in here and do your job!'

As the old lady hobbled through the kitchen door, the Cook fell back against the wall as if pushed by some unseen force.

'Gawd alive or dead! Someone cut off my nose! That's a smell that would send the devil himself back to hell!' She gasped, then staggered back into the kitchen, looking for some other ear to cuff.

Moss swiped the Abbot's soup bowl from the table and hurried to the Bell Tower. It was just past dawn. That morning, the forge had had an unexpected visit from the Armourer. Pa had shooed Moss out, but she'd not gone far and had crouched below the open shutter, where she'd heard a few snatched words. *Contraption . . . drawings . . .* And something that had sounded very much like *dragon's head,* but surely couldn't have been.

She skipped up the stairs to the Abbot's cell and waited, shuffling from foot to foot, trying to shake off the bite of frost without spilling the Abbot's breakfast. As the oak door whined open, she could see the Abbot, already at his table, head in his hands.

'Abbot?'

The man did not reply, lost in some distant thought.

'Abbot?' she said again.

He lifted his head. A shadow passed over his eyes. It startled Moss. Instinctively she took a step back. She knew that shadow. She'd seen it on the scaffold. In the eyes of men close to death.

'Who is there?'

'It's *me*. I have your soup.'

'Soup . . .' he echoed.

'Shall I wait?'

'Wait? No, no . . .' The Abbot's voice trailed to a

whisper. 'Soup . . .' He said the word tentatively, as though trying to work out its meaning.

'Shall I leave it for you? Here on the table?'

The Abbot looked up at Moss, his face blank and staring. The shadow had got him. It was a rope around his throat, pulling him away from life towards death.

'Abbot . . .'

'Is that you, Moss?'

'Yes, it's me, Abbot.' She wanted to shake him, to pull him back. But instead she forced herself to picture him. Up there on the scaffold. Pa standing over him. Moss with her basket below. She could see his face, full of confusion and fear. Here was the girl who brought his breakfast. Only this time she waited not for his soup bowl but his head.

The executions had always revolted her. But this was something else. She'd got to know the Abbot. He was a kind man. And she'd often thought her visits might bring him comfort. The thought of standing there while Pa chopped off his head made

Moss sick to her very core. She couldn't do it. She just couldn't.

The forge fire was blazing by the time Moss returned. Pa barely noticed her come in. Engrossed in his work, he didn't even look up. That suited Moss fine. She had nothing to say to him. She took a hunk of cheese from the table and put it in her pocket.

The wind chased the sounds of the water over the South Wall. With Pa occupied in the forge and a whole day ahead of her, there was nothing to stop her sneaking out right now. But something was bothering Moss. The nagging thought that made no sense, but scratched away until her head was sore with wondering. No use talking to Pa of course. But there *was* someone who might be able to help.

Checking the courtyard for any sign of Two-Bellies, she crossed quickly and trotted down the stairs to the kitchen cellars.

'Nell?'

The old lady had to be here somewhere.

'Nell? Are you there?'

From the maze of passageways came a throaty snore. Moss followed the noise until she found Nell, slumped in a corner. Three rats, very fat and very dead, were cradled in her lap.

'Nell! Wake up!'

The rags stirred, then snorted to life.

'Who goes?! Get back! I knows you're only after one thing! You'll find nothing here save an old lady in need of a little sip of ale. Good sir, do you happen to have any on you?'

'It's *me*. Moss.'

'Ah, child. Come to help this old bag of bones skin her rats?'

'If you like.'

Moss settled down beside her.

'Here, Nell. Cheese from breakfast. I couldn't get any ale, but come to the forge tonight and maybe I can sneak a little of Pa's.'

'No, no, I know when I'm not welcome. Your

father is angry with me. That song . . .'

'Oh, Nell, it was just a song. He'd no right to be angry. Anyway, he says it's all stories and superstition. He says that, but the way he acts is *scared*. He's scared of everything and I don't know why.'

Nell was quiet.

'It's not fair, Nell. He doesn't like me climbing up on the walls. He doesn't like me going near the moat. Sometimes I think he'd be happier if I was tied on a lead and never let out of his sight.'

Nell stroked the ears of one of the rats.

'I've known your father for many years. Since he carried you through the Tower gates in nothing but a blanket. I have seen him look after you and care for you as much as any mother would care for a child she loved.'

'So?'

'So you are all he has.'

'That's not true. He has his job. Here in the Tower. On the scaffold. He cleans his axe every morning. He loves that axe more than me.'

94

Nell squinted her cloudy eyes at Moss.

'In life, we do what we have to do.'

'I know, but . . .' Moss sighed. 'I just don't think *I* can do it any more.'

Nell patted Moss's knee. 'Would you like to hold one of my rats?'

'Not really, thank you, Nell.'

Moss leant back against the cellar wall and sighed.

'I still don't understand. If Pa doesn't believe in witches and ghosts and things that crawl from the river, then what's he so scared of?'

Nell drew a long breath that whistled through the gaps in her teeth.

'I daresay it's been many years since your father walked the river. Time enough for a man to forget what he once knew.'

'What? You mean he believed it all once and now he *pretends* he doesn't?'

'I mean we all have our reasons for behaving the way we do. In this world, we make our own truth.'

Moss considered this.

'Nell – do *you* think the Riverwitch is real?'

'She's as real as the cold winter current. The icy suck that pulls you down. And now –'

'What?'

'Now the fishermen say even the shore is not safe. That she walks the banks at night. Looking for a child to snatch.'

Nell cradled her rats. 'Three pretty ones. All in a row.' She looked at Moss and for a moment her cloudy eyes seemed to clear.

'No child should go near the river in winter,' said Nell. 'Your father knows that. Whether he believes the stories or not.'

A quick glance from the South Wall told Moss the tide was nearly out. The timing was perfect. The tunnel would be clear. Her heart jumped. If she judged the river right, she'd have two, maybe three hours to explore.

Her bare feet slapped on the cobbles as she made

her way to the garderobe drop. Ignoring the grunts from above, she swivelled the stone as quietly as she could and climbed through the hole.

It was easier this time. Her feet found their footholds on the steep descent. At the bottom of the well the darkness was thick, the noise of waves nothing more than a distant hum. All the same, she could feel the river. Tug-tugging. She picked her way over the flints, counting her steps, curious to know how long the tunnel was. By the time she'd reached the end, she reckoned on fifty paces.

She crawled up to the hole and began heaving the stones out one by one. Then she stopped.

Something was wrong.

The hole. It was blocked. Plugged with stones, just the way it had been when she first discovered it. Only now she thought about it, she realised *she* hadn't done it. Yesterday she'd been so spooked by the river that she'd forgotten to block the hole. But if she hadn't, then who had?

Somebody else must know about the tunnel.

Someone was using the tunnel, just like her. Well, she'd just have to be careful. Make sure she wasn't seen. Tread quietly and listen in case anyone was coming.

Squeezing her body through the gap, Moss dropped on to the shingle shore beneath the wharf and piled the stones back into place.

It was gloomy under the wharf. She crouched by the wall, looking around. Beached in the mud and tethered to a wooden pillar was a flat, pointed boat. Had it been there yesterday? Moss didn't remember seeing it. She had a quick look inside and found nothing much, just an old lantern and a sack.

All around her, the tall pillars creaked, heavy with the weight of the wooden planks above. She could hear muffled shouts from the wharf mixing with the faint rake of waves on pebbles. But now there was another noise.

Shuffle, drag. On the shingle. Something was coming.

She squinted into the murk. A shadow moved

under the wharf.

Instinctively, Moss darted behind one of the pillars and pressed herself against it, holding her breath, trying not to make a sound. She could feel her heart beating a pulse all the way up her throat. Pa had always told her the penalty for anyone caught trying to escape the Tower was death. She tried to swallow, but her mouth was dry.

Closer came the noise. *Shuffle, drag.* Like the limp of an injured foot.

And now a strange feeling crept down Moss's back, pricking her skin, snatching her breath. She could not explain it. Just that it made her want to run. She pressed herself flatter against the pillar, willing the steps to pass her by, wishing she was anywhere but here where her body crawled with the dread of a thing she did not understand.

The damp air filled with a smell that scraped the back of her throat. A heady, choking smell, like a pig that had been left too long on the spit. And now she heard a metallic sound. The chink of coins.

Then it stopped. Moss blinked. Everything was silent. All she could hear was the distant lap of waves on the shore. Slowly, carefully, she peeked out from behind the pillar. There was no one there.

Suddenly a hand shot from the darkness and seized her by the neck, dragging her backwards.

Moss's scream stuck in her mouth. From behind her came a hiss.

'And who would miss *you*, I wonder?'

A man's voice. His face so close she could feel the heat from his skin.

'Get off me!' She tore at his hands, but his grip was fierce and he pressed the hollow at the base of her throat until she thought she would choke. Still she could not see him. His breath was on her cheek.

'Ah, the Executioner's daughter . . .'

Moss's eyes were popping. How did he know who she was?

'All alone under a dark wharf.' The man's whispered words hung in the dank air. 'Not yet for you, but soon enough . . .'

Twisting her body wildly, Moss kicked out. As her foot made contact, she heard the clatter of coins spilling on to the pebbles and the grip on her neck went slack. She wrenched her body free. Just for a second, before she ran, she saw his face. Hooded and covered by a cracked black mask.

Moss tore over the shingle, lunging towards daylight, scrabbling out from under the wharf. Her breaths were ragged and her throat throbbed where the man's fingers had pressed. She could still hear his rasping voice. *Not yet for you, but soon enough . . .* What did he mean? She tried to smother the hiss that slithered through her head, but could not.

She should go back. Now. To the safety of the forge and Pa.

Moss closed her eyes and drew the river air into her lungs. Her breathing steadied.

At that moment, a splinter of sunlight poked through the clouds and she felt her spirits lift. She couldn't go back. Not yet. This was her chance. To venture into the wide world outside. She would go on. Explore, just a little. She had until the tide turned. And as long as she didn't stray from the shore, she wouldn't get lost.

There was no sign of the man. Still, she couldn't help glancing over her shoulder every few steps to check he wasn't following her.

She hurried along the shingle away from the wharf, past the jumble of huts, past big timbered houses with little jetties and their own flights of stairs threading their way down to the water. Moss was almost tempted to climb them, but she supposed they were not meant for barefoot girls like her. She didn't want to risk drawing attention to herself, so she stayed on the shingle.

Before her stretched the Thames, broken only by the towering bulk of London Bridge. She counted the massive stone arches. There were nineteen, looping across the river. Each was planted on a wide pointed plinth, like the fat, staggering legs of a child. Seeing this bridge close up for the first time, Moss couldn't help but wonder how it stayed up. Rickety buildings were stacked along the length of it, some three or four floors high. There were houses and shops and even a chapel, its elegant spire soaring above the tumbling roofs. And the noise! Even from the shore, it was deafening. Workmen banging. The cry of merchants. A maid yelling at a servant who had tipped his master's pot from a high window. Moss heard carts rattling along the road towards it and the thump of soldiers' feet marching off it. It was a bridge that heaved and groaned like a living thing. And now she was close, more than anything Moss wanted to be up there too.

She clambered up the steep steps to the bridge road. She'd be quick – just one little walk to the end and back.

'Out of the way, yer damn fool girl!'

Moss skipped sideways as a cart jumping with barrels thundered past. Another followed it, shedding cabbages as it jolted over the rough mud road. A herd of cows followed the carts, trampling the cabbages, their rumps twitching as a drover beat them with a stick. Then came the crack and grind of a carriage, churning up the mud with its fallen vegetables and chicken feathers and a muddy lump that could have been a sack or a cat.

Moss breathed in and stepped into the crush. Instantly she was swept forward. Staggering, she struggled to stay on her feet, darting behind a drayman to walk in the wake of his cart. The drayman whipped his horse through the tollgate and Moss followed, staring at the timbered buildings that leered on either side.

Through the great stone arch, the bridge was a narrow covered street, darkened from above by passageways that linked the tall buildings. The crowd shoved its way forward and Moss had the strange sensation of being squeezed like meat into one of Mrs Peak's sausage skins. All around her, shopkeepers beckoned, hawkers shouted, people argued and merchants unrolled rich cloth from windows above.

Moss scrambled out of the flowing crowd and

clung to the side of a shop. Her wide eyes blinked. She hoped that no one would think her strange. Everything was so close and unfamiliar. How different it was from the discipline and the grey stone of the Tower. So much laughter and anger without anyone really taking the slightest bit of notice. She felt so far away from her normal life it made her want to laugh out loud. And no one would have minded if she had.

Moss set off again. It couldn't be much further to the end of the bridge. Under her bare feet, the mud became rough wood. Through the gaps in wooden planks she could see the river tearing through the arches below. And all at once, Moss realised where she was.

Her stomach twisted. She couldn't help herself. She turned and looked up. Above her loomed the smooth stone towers of the Drawbridge Gate. Spiked to its turrets were the heads. Traitors' heads. Withered, cheeks fallen, eyes long gone, some with tongues hanging out as if tasting the salt air.

Moss's life rushed back at her. In less than a week, the head of the Abbot would be up there with them. Withering with the rest as a lesson to others. Chopped by Pa. Carried down the hill in a basket by Moss.

Not this time. No matter what Pa said. Sure as rats have tails. She would not do it.

CHAPTER TEN
The Ragged Man

Tower people always said the first two months of the year were the harshest. But this year there was something about the cold that had them muttering more than usual. The winter wind blew wild off the river. Anyone who got in its way was whipped as soundly as a kitchen boy on a feast day.

Moss had stayed away from the tunnel. She'd spent restless nights, her dreams haunted by the hiss of the man under the wharf, waking suddenly in the darkness to listen for his shuffling step. But there was no one. The hissing man wasn't there, though there wasn't enough comfort in that thought to get back to sleep.

It was morning. Pa had woken Moss early. For the last few days, he'd sent her out of the forge as soon as she'd returned from the kitchen. Given her bread and cheese and told her to leave him to work alone until supper. That suited Moss just fine. But she had to admit, she was curious to know what he'd been doing. So this morning, when he'd shooed her out, she'd skulked outside the forge until she could hear the chink of his hammer. Now she crept back in. Pa stood on the other side of the raised brick fireplace that occupied the middle of the room. He was working at the anvil with his back to her. He was concentrating, she could tell. Hammering with short, rhythmic taps, his bulk blocking whatever it was he was making.

Quietly she crept towards the fireplace. He could not hear her.

Chink, chink went the hammer.

Moss was at the fireplace now, crouching behind the brick wall. Peeping over the top. Craning to see what it was he was hammering. Just as she was about to slide round to the other side, Pa turned and thrust a huge piece of metal into the embers. A flurry of sparks and flames crackled to the roof and Moss nearly fell backwards.

'Oh!'

She was staring into the open jaws of a hideous beast, jagged with dagger-sharp metal teeth.

'Christ!' Pa jumped back, startled by Moss's cry. Then he plunged the jaws into the water bucket and they hissed, filling the forge with steam.

He turned to face her. 'What are you doing here? I thought you'd gone.'

'What *is* that thing?'

'It's nothing. Just some . . . some new-fangled armour for . . . for a captain's horse. And it doesn't concern you.'

'But –'

'But nothing. It's extra work. Perhaps it'll pay for new boots.'

'Better than taking money from a dead man,' muttered Moss.

'I'm sorry?'

'I *said*, better than taking money from a man on the scaffold who's as good as dead.'

'What are you talking about?'

'You know what I'm talking about. You just go along with it. It's blood money. And it makes me sick.'

Pa frowned at Moss. 'It's the custom and you know it.'

'Anyway, I bet the Abbot hasn't got two farthings to rub together. If he can't pay, what then?'

Pa's laid his hammer and tongs on the anvil.

'A man deserves a good, clean death, whoever he is, whatever the weight of his purse.'

'Oh, how honourable of you. You chop off a man's head. In front of that screaming crowd. And you call it a good death?'

'We've been through this, Moss –'

'Yes! We have! So what's the point? There's never any point trying to talk to you. You don't listen to me. You just do what *you* think. I might as well not be here. So you can find someone else to carry that damned basket!'

Pa stared at Moss, too surprised to speak.

'Go on then,' said Moss, waiting for him to pick up his hammer. 'Just carry on. Just carry on like you always do.'

She turned her back on Pa and walked out.

There was no way she was carrying that basket for the Abbot's execution. Someone else would have to catch the Abbot's head and she didn't care who.

By dusk, the freezing fog was curling over the walls and Moss could barely feel her toes. The mood in the kitchen was sombre as she arrived to take the Abbot his last meal. There'd be no breakfast tomorrow. Lieutenant's orders. Ever since the Bishop had thrown up all over the scaffold, and all over the Lieutenant's new buckled shoes. No breakfast for the prisoner on Execution Day.

Mrs Peak fussed over the plate before shoving it into Moss's hands.

'Half a chicken. With lemons. And if anyone says the Tower kitchen doesn't do a decent last supper then I'm Pope Paul.'

The chicken did smell good and Moss was glad for the Abbot's sake. But as she waited for the guard to open his cell door, she wondered whether he'd have the stomach for it.

Wrapped in his prayers, the Abbot didn't even look up. A hearty blaze was roaring in the fireplace. Warm, fed and quiet. There were worse ways to spend your last night, thought Moss. She remembered his kindness and how he'd talked with her these past days. She looked at the Abbot's straggling hair and remembered the heads on the bridge. She hoped that when his moment came he would be steady, that he'd close his eyes and think of the woods and the mistle thrush and forget the baying crowd on Tower Hill.

She set the plate of chicken on the table, glad that *this* would be her last memory of the Abbot. Bent in prayer. In a room that smelt of spiced lemons. Not a lolling, bloody head in her basket.

'Goodbye, Abbot,' she whispered, turning as she walked for the last time through his cell door.

The curfew bell was clanging as Moss hurried down the steps of the Bell Tower. The biting wind had made sure that no one stayed out longer than they had to and the courtyard was empty. Moss padded quietly past Traitors' Gate. She could hear the slop of moat water against the wooden grille, but as she got nearer, she heard something else.

Voices. Whispering voices. Coming from the stone steps that led to the gate.

'Where is he then? Should have been here by now.'

'He'll come, don't you worry.'

'I'm tellin you, Ned, he gives me the ghosts.'

'Shut it, Laces.'

Moss slipped herself against the wall, inching slowly forward to see who was there.

Two soldiers. She could just make out their faces in the fading light, anxious and fixed on Traitors' Gate.

'I don't like it, Ned. Not one bit. He creeps about the place. Never see him come, never see him go. Unless he's on his boat, bringin' in them sacks.'

The other soldier grunted.

'I've started seein him in me dreams, Ned. Creepin an' hissin an' *burnin.*'

'I *said*, put a lid on it, Laces.'

'And what's under that mask of his, Ned? Ever asked yerself that?'

'I don't know an' I don't want to know.'

'Death, that's what. He's the dead come walkin, Ned.'

'Dead men don't need money though, do they?'

There was a sudden slap of water against the gate and the sound of oars, carrying from the moat.

'Here he comes!'

Moss jumped into the dark shadow of the Bloody Tower and tucked herself behind a pile of barrels. She heard the creak of the water gate and the clatter of a boat coming to rest against the stone steps.

Up the steps came the two soldiers humping a large sack. A third man walked behind, his face shrouded by a drooping hood. Moss could see his cloak was ragged, his back was bent and he walked with some difficulty. He carried a lantern, orange light flickering over the cobbles.

The soldiers heaved the sack to the door of the Bloody Tower and set it down on the cobbles.

'Money now, ragged man,' said one of the soldiers.

The man turned slowly towards the soldier. Moss peered through the gap in the barrels, but still could not see his face.

'Money first,' said the soldier. But his voice was a little less certain. 'That was –'

'Our deal? And what would you know about deals, you who *betrayed* me?' hissed the man.

It was a voice that stirred a memory in Moss's

brain. Her breath quickened and a strange feeling pricked the skin on her back.

The soldiers did not argue and Moss could see in their faces that they were afraid of the one they called the ragged man.

'So . . .' The ragged man spoke with contempt in his voice. 'A shilling I will pay you now. The rest at high tide tomorrow.'

He opened a large pouch that hung from his belt and Moss heard the chink of coins.

As the soldiers counted their money, there was another sound, picking away at the shadows under the arch of the Bloody Tower. A scratching noise. So faint, it could have been a mouse. It was coming from the sack. The sack, Moss realised, was just inches from the pile of barrels where she crouched.

Slowly, gently, she eased herself on to all fours and crawled towards it. She was pretty sure the soldiers could not see her. All the same, she moved carefully, grateful for the shadows and for the failing light. Now she was close. And Moss could see the sack was moving very slightly.

What was in there? Ducks? It was an odd time of night to be trapping ducks. Odder still to be bringing them in through Traitors' Gate.

The corner of the sack was still moving. Rippling slightly with little bumps pushing outwards. As gently as she could, Moss reached out to touch it. Through the cloth she felt something firm, knobbly. Then something grabbed her finger.

For a moment she froze, her finger trapped by the thing in the sack. She yanked her hand back, stifling a cry. That was no duck.

It had felt very much . . . *like a hand.*

Moss shrank back behind the barrels. She heard the door to the Bloody Tower swing open. The soldiers grunted as they heaved the sack off the cobbles. Then they were gone. In the air was a lingering smell. Of char and burn. A smell she knew, all around her now, scraping the back of her throat.

Not yet for you, but soon enough . . .

It was him, she was sure of it. The man who'd seized her under the wharf.

The *ragged man*.

He was here. In the Tower.

CHAPTER ELEVEN
Truth and Lies

Whack!

The axe hit its mark. But before Moss could stop it, the head had missed her basket and was rolling down the hill. She dropped the basket and ran, chasing the head as it tumbled. Faster rolled the head. Faster she ran. But she couldn't catch it. It was rolling down one side of the hill towards the Tower. Then something flashed in the corner of her eye on the other side of the hill. The river. Moss stopped running. *The river.* She turned and began to walk towards it. But suddenly there was Pa. Holding his axe like a quarterstaff. Blocking her way. She wanted to get near that river. He didn't move. So she ripped the axe from his hands and flung it as high as she could, as far as she could. She watched it cartwheel through the sky . . .

Bang!

Moss awoke just in time to see her flailing arm send the water jug clattering to the floor. She blinked and the vision of the axe melted away.

She always had that dream on Execution Day.

Moss looked round the forge. Pa was nowhere to be seen. He was probably out by the main gate, loading the Executioner's block on to the cart to be taken up the hill. She was quite alone. Clutching her blanket, she listened, half expecting to hear the shuffle of that ragged man. Only when she was sure she was quite alone did she climb off her pallet, trying to shake all thought of him from her head.

There was extra cheese on the table and a leg of mutton. Moss bit into the mutton and stuffed the cheese in her dress pocket. She reckoned if she set off now, she'd be able to get out and miss the whole execution and still be back before the tunnel flooded.

In the corner, something made her stop. A glint of something.

Pa's axe. He hadn't taken it with him yet. The sackcloth cover had come loose, exposing the wide end of the blade.

Moss walked over and poked it with her toe. She hated that axe. Hated how Pa polished it every morning, hated that it was always there in the corner of the forge, reminding her what Pa was, what *she* was.

She gave it a kick and it clanged to the floor.

That felt good.

She kicked it again, half hoping to bring Pa racing in, shouting at her. Just so she could shout back. And then a thought occurred to her. A dangerous thought.

Quickly, Moss picked up the axe and wrapped it

tightly in the sackcloth. She poked her head out of the forge door. Checking Pa was nowhere in sight, she hobbled out on to the Green, keeping close to the walls. By the time she reached the garderobe drop, her arms were aching from the weight.

She lugged the axe down the steps and into the drop. As she heaved back the stone that hid the way to the tunnel, she heard someone settling into position in the garderobe above. Not wanting to be spattered, she shoved herself through the gap, dragging the axe behind her. She repositioned the stone and stopped to listen.

Silence. She was alone in the darkness.

It took all Moss's strength to get the axe down to the bottom. Clinging to the footholds with one hand, twice she nearly lost her grip. By the time she reached the tunnel, her arms were fit to drop from their sockets.

There was water in the tunnel. Shin-deep. Moss picked up her skirts and bundled the axe up with them. The tide was on its way out, just as she had calculated. Good. She'd have more time on the outside.

At the tunnel's end, she pushed out as many stones as she could, letting them drop into the water, then squeezed her slight frame through, pulling the axe after her. It was no easy task, trying to keep her dress out of the water while reblocking the hole. The current tugged at her legs as she bent down, freezing hands groping for the stones. By the time she'd finished, Moss was exhausted.

She waded out from under the wharf. The morning fog had not yet gone. It lay heavy on the retreating river, thick as Mrs Peak's broth. On mornings like these, most boats stayed in their berths until the sun had burned it away. Many times from the battlements Moss had heard the cries of men and the splintering of wood as hasty ships collided in the fog. Fog was the enemy of all sailors. But here, today, for a girl wading to the shore with an axe in her arms, it hid her from curious eyes.

The handle was worn smooth. She could almost

feel Pa's hands round it. She knew he'd be angry that she'd taken it. She *wanted* him to be angry. Let him shout at her. She'd shout back.

Moss gripped the axe and staggered back. Swinging it in a wide arc over her head, she hurled it with all the force she could manage. She watched it cartwheel into the sky – a strange, ungainly whirling before it disappeared into the fog. It landed in the river with a satisfying splash. Up in the sky, beyond the swirling mists, she heard the shriek of gulls and felt like shrieking with them.

She'd worked out that she had until about midday before the tide turned back and began to flood the tunnel once again. Time enough to wander up and explore the narrow streets if she felt brave enough. The fog would lift soon. Then she would go.

From somewhere out on the river, Moss heard the pat of oars. A small craft, by the sound of it. Moss remembered her boots and half wondered whether she might find the thieving river boy. She peered out over the water.

The point of a thin, flat boat poked out of the mist. It was travelling parallel to the shore, but the mist was so thick, she couldn't make out who was rowing it. Maybe it was the boot thief.

Moss jumped up. She walked quickly, keeping pace with the shadowy boat until it was close to London Bridge. There it disappeared completely into the swirling fog. She stopped walking and listened. In the distance, somewhere out there on the river, was a strange, high-pitched ringing. Like the tinkling of a small bell. And the river grew suddenly calm. Unnaturally calm.

Now she could hear a whimpering. Out on the river somewhere. And the chink of a hammer on stone. Then the pat of oars again and the water was silent.

A sudden cry and a splash broke the silence. She could hear thrashing in the water. In front of her, the river began to churn. Then it stopped. The water was calm again. There was a cracking noise, like the splintering of glass, and Moss saw fingers of frost shooting from the shore across the river, leaving a trail of ice behind them.

She blinked. Trapped in the frozen water were shining coins. Gold and silver, embedded in the ice like jewels in a crown. She took a step into the river. Fog swirled all around her. As she gasped at the cold that clenched her ankles, she heard the slap of oars coming towards her and backed away.

The flat, pointed boat was coming to shore. And the creep down her spine told her she should not be there when it arrived.

Two long hours Moss spent, shivering on the steps of Tower Wharf waiting for the execution to finish, trying to make sense of what she'd seen and heard. The tinkling bell. The churning river. And the coins embedded in the ice. Had she really seen those? Or imagined the whole thing? Maybe the fog was playing tricks on her eyes.

Boom! Boom!

The cannons were firing. That meant the execution was done.

Moss scrambled back under the wharf. Suddenly all she could think about was getting back to the warm forge.

On Tower Green, the kitchen girls were watching the last of the soldiers marching through the arch. There was no sign of Pa. Moss scooted round the White Tower to the forge and banged open the door.

'Pa!'

Pa hauled her inside and rapped the door shut.

'I knew you'd be angry,' said Moss, trying to jump in before he got started. 'The axe –'

'Forget the axe.' Pa's face was white. 'Where have you been?'

'I . . . I – Ow!' Pa was gripping her arm, tight as a shackle. There was something about his expression. It frightened her. And it stopped the words that were all set to tumble out of her mouth.

'I said, where have you been!'

'Nowhere.'

'Don't lie to me! I looked everywhere for you. I've been out of my mind with worry. *Where have you been?*'

The rage of the past six months. The heads. The blood. The way Pa just got on with their miserable life, all welled up in Moss.

'Get off me! GET OFF ME!'

She tried to yank her arm free, but Pa held on tight.

'Listen. I don't know what's got into you and I'm not even going to start on the axe, but you get this into that stubborn head of yours and you get it in now. I need to know where you are. Especially on a day like today. When the gates open, I need you by my side. With that basket. Not hiding up in some dark corner of a tower. I am a prisoner here. If I put a foot wrong, I may not *have* a foot by the morning. And you are a prisoner too. Like it or not.'

'Not!' yelled Moss.

Pa tightened his grip. 'I killed a man.' His voice was feverish. 'By rights I should have swung. But they let me live. Now I cut off heads. I do as good a job as I can. And I don't complain. Because if I do, I hang.'

'You don't fool me! You like it here, don't you?'

'What are you talking about?'

'You polish your axe, you stoke your fire, you never look beyond these walls. You had a life once. A life outside. And I guess that was enough for you. But I *never* had that. And if you get *your* way I never will. Have you *any idea* what that feels like?'

Moss felt Pa's grip slacken and she wrenched herself away.

'Moss . . .' Pa hesitated. 'It just isn't possible.'

'What's not possible? For you to stop for one minute and think about something that matters? Not whether we've got mutton for supper. Not polishing your damned axe!'

'Everything I've done, I did for you. There can be no life outside for us.' Pa's voice was steady, but his hands were trembling. She tried to read his face. There was worry and pain there, and a faraway look that she recognised from the times she'd tried to ask about her mother. It frightened her to see him like this. She wished they were still arguing.

Pa slumped in a chair and gestured for her to sit opposite him at the table.

'I should have told you long ago, I knew I should. But . . . you're still just a girl.'

'That's stupid. In two and a half weeks I'll be *twelve*.'

What little colour there was left in Pa's ashen face drained away.

'Twelve . . .' He stopped, as if to listen for the echo of his own voice. 'Twelve.' He took her face in his shaking hands. 'When your mother died, I promised I would keep you safe. That day, the day you were born, something was done. Something that cannot be undone.'

All her years, Moss had been waiting for this moment. To know what had happened. How her mother had died. Yet now Pa was talking, she almost didn't want to hear.

'We were running, your ma and I. The soldiers were coming. They had horses. We could hear them behind us. We'd been running for days. She thought she was slowing me down, you see. Your ma. I carried her as far as I could, but she was heavy with the baby . . .' He faltered. 'With *you* inside her.'

Moss tried to picture herself inside her mother. It was impossible to think of herself this way. Unborn. Unseen by her ma or pa.

'We had to stop. Both of us knew we couldn't run any more. Then I heard the whistle of willows and thought we might be near a river.'

'A river? The river where I was born?' asked Moss.

Pa nodded. 'It was cold that day. A frostbitten February. The end of a cold winter. But I wasn't thinking about the cold. I thought . . . I thought, maybe the river could save us?' He pressed his thumb into his temple as though trying to push the thought back in. 'I was wrong.

'There was an old mill. A ruin. A crooked chimney sitting on a pile of grey tumbling stone.

Overgrown, with willows on the bank and a cracked waterwheel that looked like it hadn't turned for centuries. The water was dark and silent behind that stopped wheel. A hiding place, I thought. So I took your ma's hand. I told her to jump. And we jumped. Into the water.'

Although she'd never seen her mother, Moss tried to imagine her there, with Pa, holding his hand. She gave her wavy chestnut hair and the dimple from her own right cheek. She heard her gasp as she hit the water.

'It was so cold,' said Pa. 'A crust of ice shattered as we fell through. The shock of it . . . The baby – you – began to come. And . . .'

'And what?'

'You were coming too fast.'

Moss knew enough about childbirth to know too fast was a dangerous thing. She'd watched Ella from the kitchens as she'd had her baby and she'd heard the women say it was too soon and too quick and they were doing all they could, but it most likely wouldn't be enough for poor Ella. Moss pictured Ma now, screaming, her body twisting and arching like Ella's. She could see her ma's blood, seeping from under her dress into the water, like thick red smoke.

'I couldn't move,' said Pa. 'The freezing river seemed to have me in its grip and your mother . . . She was gasping, struggling. I was losing her. And the baby. I don't know why she did it, but she screamed for help. Your mother cried out. I hoped to goodness the soldiers hadn't heard her. Then I thought I must be dreaming because from under that old wheel, out of the water, rose a woman. Her face was weather-worn, pale as ice. Her dress was like weeds. I suppose she was strange, but she said she could help. Yet there was a coldness to her words and I could sense that this offer was not one of kindness. *We don't want your help*, I said.

'*Yes Sam, we do*, whispered your mother. Her breaths were faint like a little bird. *I'm dying*, she said. *And if I die our child dies too* . . .'

Pa trailed off and rubbed his eye. 'The river woman spoke to your mother. *You asked for my help. And I will give it.* But there was ice in her voice. And then . . .' Pa hesitated. 'And then she said, *Your life I cannot save, but your child, your daughter, perhaps . . .*

'*Daughter?* said your ma, her eyes soft with wonder. *Our baby is a girl? Please. Save her if you can.*

'*I will save the baby,* said the woman. *But know this. A child that is born to the river shall return to the river. Twelve years you shall have. To love her. To hold her. After that, the river daughter . . . she belongs to me.*'

Moss stared at Pa, trying to take in, to make sense of, what he was telling her.

'Who was she, this river woman?'

Pa's voice cracked to a whisper. '*She seeks the thing she'll never have. A loving child to hold . . .*'

Nell's song. The song of the river.

Moss took a step back from Pa. He was staring at her wildly.

'The Riverwitch.' His words cut through her, dagger-deep.

'*What?* But – you don't even believe! Superstition
. . . You said –'

'I know what I said. Listen to me now.' Pa was
talking quickly and some of his words were tangled,
as though they'd been put away for a long time and
never sorted through. 'Your mother was dying. She
would have done anything, *anything* to save you.'

Tears began to spill from his eyes and the sight of
them made Moss want to turn away.

'*Don't leave me*, I whispered to your mother. *Don't
. . . die. Stay with me . . .* But she just said, *Promise me
you will look after our child. Do what you can to keep
her.* I could feel her slipping away. So I begged that
creature. *Take me instead.*'

Tears were flowing freely now from Pa's eyes,
little salt rivers down his ash-stained cheeks. 'But
the woman shook her head. *Only the child.*'

Moss saw her mother, lying in Pa's arms in that
dark place. Fighting for breath while the water grew
redder. She pictured her own tiny hands breaking
the surface of the water. Her mother reaching for

her baby. And though it was just a picture in her head, Moss willed time to stop. To feel the comfort of her mother's arms. Her warm breath. But now she saw her father's broken face. And instead of her mother's soft embrace, she felt frost fingers pluck her from the water.

'If I could go back. If I hadn't made her jump into that godforsaken river.' Pa's bloodshot eyes searched Moss's face. 'I promised her. I promised I would keep you safe.'

But all Moss could see was her mother's body floating by the millwheel. And blood. So much blood. Caught by the current, carried past the willows, their branches trailing in the pink water.

Pa was still talking. 'The soldiers caught up with me. They flogged me for what I'd done and left me. And for a year I wandered from village to village with you, doing any job I could find to feed and clothe you . . .'

Lost in her thoughts, Moss was barely listening to Pa now. But something jerked her back.

'Wait,' she said, '*flog* you? You told me you should have hanged. You said you were on the run for killing a man in your regiment.'

Pa rubbed his face. 'I told you that, but it wasn't true. I stole from a man. I didn't kill him. And perhaps they would have cut off my hand for that. But when they found me with your mother and the baby they took pity, I suppose. They beat me, but that was all. Then I brought you here. I heard they were having trouble with their Executioners. Too many botched beheadings. They needed someone who could do the job clean and quick. I offered myself. And you have to believe me when I say that what I do on Tower Hill makes me sick to my stomach.'

'So . . . So . . .' Slowly Moss began to make sense of Pa's words. 'So *you* brought *me* to the Tower. You *pretended* we were prisoners here?'

'It was the only way I could think to keep you safe.'

'All this time?' Moss could barely believe what she was hearing. 'You *lied* to me? You brought me up in this . . . in this place? You made me carry that basket? You *pretended* we were prisoners?'

'I had to keep you away from the river. Away from all rivers. I promised your mother. To keep you safe.' He touched her hand and Moss flinched.

All these years. She could have walked out *any time*. She would have laughed if she wasn't so angry. Pa had lied to her. He had imprisoned her. His own daughter.

Pa was talking, but Moss barely heard.

'In two weeks you will be twelve. You can see, can't you, why we must stay here? Here, away from the rivers, where that . . . that creature can't get you. I can't lose you too, Moss.'

Moss backed away. Her mother was dead. Her father was a liar. Her father was her jailer.

'Get away from me,' she whispered.

Moss pushed past Pa. She kicked open the door and walked out.

CHAPTER TWELVE
Leaving

Moss's hands were shaking as she shoved the last stone into the hole at the end of the tunnel.

At the river's edge she stood now. Alone. Her heart beating so loud she could hear it thumping off the wharf wall. Behind her was the Tower. Everything and everyone she knew was in that place.

Executioner. *Liar.*

It was *the lie* that got her the most. She couldn't shake it from her head. They had never been prisoners. Pa had lied to her all this time. Hidden her away. From what? From something that had happened twelve years ago. A crazy old river woman? A Riverwitch? A ghost?

Well, she would hide no more. She was leaving. It was all she'd ever wanted and now there was nothing to stop her.

The wind blew the choppy waves back and forth. Beckoning her. Pushing her back.

Walk, she told herself. But her feet wouldn't move.

Get away from me. Those had been her last words to Pa. Now they choked her throat.

Walk, she told herself again. But her legs were stone.

What was out there? She knew no one. Nothing. And as she stared at the endless grey river, fear prised her head open, filling it with dark thoughts. The haunted face of Pa. Her dying mother. The shuffling steps of the ragged man. She could hear his hiss, feel his fingers pressing on her neck. Moss clutched her throat and staggered against the wall.

Silence. She heard nothing but the waves stroking the shore.

'Walk!' This time she said it out loud. And the dark inside brightened a little at the sound of her own voice. Moss's feet burned cold on the shingle. But she was walking now.

Where would she go? All by herself. Without Pa.

In her imaginings of a life outside, she'd always pictured herself and Pa in a little village somewhere. The kind of place Nell had told her about. A chalky hillside or a bluebell wood. A beautiful place, far away from the Tower. But now these visions faded, replaced by something more powerful, tugging at her from deep within.

Into her head drifted Nell's lilting words. The song of the river. Now she knew why it had made Pa so angry. It had stirred up memories he'd buried deep. So deep, he'd almost been able to forget they were there. But they were *her* memories too. What happened that day, in the water beside the mill.

The mill . . .

Moss stopped walking.

'The mill?'

She would look for that old mill. The place she was born. The place where her mother had died. Maybe she'd find a crazy river woman. Or a ghost. Or the lingering voice of her mother? Whatever, she'd find her *own* memories, not Pa's. In the place where she'd begun.

What had Nell called it? Hampton? The Hampton Wheel. On a bend of this very river, Nell had said. But was it up- or downriver? Moss had no idea.

'All right then. Up.' She would walk upriver. She would ask people along the way. But a walk of any distance could not be done in bare feet. She needed her boots. So she needed to find that thieving boy.

Creasing her eyes, she scanned the river. It was a fogless day and shouts from the water carried all the way to shore. Moss could hear *everything*. The laughter of deckhands on the big ships and the filthy language of the watermen who rowed their passengers in wobbling boats. But there was no sign of that boy thief. Slowly, she made her way along the shoreline, scouring the river until her eyeballs ached.

The tide was out. Everywhere was mud. Thin figures, like wisps of smoke, drifted between the huts on the banks. Some had lit fires in shallow pits and she could see people crouching for warmth. As she got closer, Moss realised they were mostly children, wearing shabby garments that hung stiff with dirt. One drifted close to her. A girl, her face hungry. The child stared up at Moss with sunken eyes, lashes so threadbare they looked like they might blow away in the breeze.

'What's yer problem? Village lost its idiot today then?'

Moss wheeled round and there he was. The thief was walking towards her, dragging his wooden boat behind him through the mud.

Moss swallowed.

'Go home, rich girl. There's nothin fer you here.'

'*Rich girl?* You mean me?'

He cocked his dirt-smudged face to one side and pointed at his feet. They were planted firmly inside her boots. 'Whoever bought these ain't short of a groat or two.'

Moss didn't quite know what to say. But glancing around at the hungry children, she could see why her boots might seem like something worth having.

'We're not rich. Pa worked hard for those boots. Shod the Armourer's horses, then pulled two of his wife's teeth.'

The thief laughed. 'Blacksmith, eh? Nice work if you can get it.' He began hauling his boat over the mud ruts towards a cluster of huts.

'Wait!'

'Great Harry's pussin ulcers! You followin me, shore girl?'

'No, I mean *yes*. I mean I want my boots back.'

'They're *my* boots now.'

The thief dropped his boat next to a low shack, a patchwork of driftwood, planks and sackcloth.

Was that where he lived? It was barely bigger than a dog kennel.

Around her now the threadbare children crowded. They didn't touch her. They said nothing, just stood, stick-limbed, sunken-eyed.

Moss reached into her pocket and felt the broken pieces of the cheese she'd taken from the forge that morning. It was all the food she had. But these children, they were so thin they were hardly there at all.

Slowly, she brought her hand out of her pocket. With their pale eyes, the children followed her every move. She opened her palm. In it was the yellow, crumbled cheese. The children looked from the cheese to Moss and back to the cheese, as though the very sight of it might nourish them.

Moss held out her palm. 'Go on,' she said gently. 'You can have it. It's good.'

Little fingers plucked the pieces from her hand. Held the food to their lips and nibbled, eyes wide, like mice. A few feet away, the boy watched from behind his upturned boat. He stowed his oars underneath. Then he disappeared inside the shack without looking back.

The wind was picking up now, drawing out the twilight cries of the streets. From the huts that dotted the banks, men and women called their children in. Their voices pierced the dusk, tight with fear.

'Get in, get in! Dark's comin and the shore ain't no place for lingerin children!'

Nell was right. The fishermen were afraid of something. And superstition or not, Moss had a problem. Night was coming and she had nowhere to sleep. Maybe she should have asked that thief. Pleaded for a corner of his shack. But what would that make her? Beggar? Prisoner? What was the difference? Either way you had no self-respect.

Moss trudged along the shore, wondering whether she should head into the city to find some kind of shelter. She looked up at the lines of shadowy houses and the narrow streets that closed in around them. The thought of losing sight of the

146

river scared her more than anything. Here outside the Tower, the river was all she knew.

She hadn't come far. Just halfway to the bridge. The air reeked of putrid fish, and she noticed nets and piles of boxes heaped on the shore above the tidemark. Dragging the largest she could find up on to the bank, Moss kicked out the fish debris and tucked herself inside. It stank, but at least she was a bit further from the water and maybe it would keep out the wind.

Hours later, Moss was still awake,. her teeth chattering so violently she thought they might break. She had never been so cold.

She closed her eyes and willed her body to let sleep come.

CHAPTER THIRTEEN
Salter

It was a surprise when she opened her eyes several hours later and saw that it was getting light. What's more she was almost warm. A musty sack covered her.

Moss sat up and banged her head. 'Ow!'

She poked her head into the grey outside and blinked. Guarding the entrance to the box were her boots.

By the time she found his shack again, the thief was already up. He sat on a stone, stuffing straw into the sole of a shoe that was more hole than leather. Beside him was his net, trailing riverweed and glistening with the bodies of silver fish.

'Still here?' He pulled on the shoe and began binding a piece of cloth round the other foot, packing in more straw before drawing his ankle tight with twine.

Moss wasn't sure what to say. She could see the boy needed her boots almost as much as she did and wished she had something to offer in exchange.

'Can you gut?' said the boy.

'What?'

'Can you gut a fish?'

'I . . . can't. No.'

He frowned. 'Can't gut no fish, can't swim. Bout as much use as a dead rat's bum.'

She watched him shake out the contents of his net and arrange ten skinny fish side by side, their spangled scales glinting like armour.

'Are you going to cook those fish?'

The boy nodded.

'I can light a fire.'

No response. Had he heard her? 'I can light a fire. If you like?'

'Kindlin's in the box, wood's in the sack.'

It didn't take Moss long to get a good blaze going. The boy's fire pit was lined with pebbles, raising it out of the mud. The kindling, an assortment of paper-thin seaweed and dry bulrush stems, took the flint sparks like gunpowder. Now Moss laid the driftwood, drawing the flames inwards until the centre was a pillar of fire. The boy poked three silver fish into the embers and tied the others by their tails to a stick. Then he tossed some smoking charcoal into a narrow hole next to the pit, layered it with wood shavings, suspended the fish-stick above and covered the whole thing with a large flat stone.

'What's that?'

'Smoker. I smokes the sprats, sells what I don't eat meself.'

'Are you a fisherman?'

'Nah. Waterman. I ferries folks from bank to bank.'

'Oh?'

'Know every stretch of this old river. An' I've had em all in me boat – fat lords, black-toothed ladies, dogs with earrings . . . Course, *you* wouldn't know about an honest day's work, Miss Leatherboots.'

'Honest? What's honest about robbing a drowning person?'

'Think I should have left you fer the fishes?'

'No decent person would steal from a half-drowned girl.'

'Decent.' The boy looked amused. 'Decent.' He rolled the word around his tongue. 'Decent don't really come into it round here. Guess you blacksmiths' girls ain't scrappin for every morsel, if you got time to be so good to one another.' He was mocking her again, but this time his eyes crinkled, little crow's feet making lines through his dirt-smudged cheeks.

The sprats hissed in the embers, their skins popping.

'Here.' The boy dragged one out of the fire.

It was hot and crispy and smelt delicious. Moss couldn't remember a time when she had eaten a fish just cooked. Scraps from the night before maybe, but never a fresh, hot fish like this, cooked simply in a fire. The smell drew some of the younger children from nearby hovels. As they crept closer, the boy pulled a sprat into pieces for them, which they gnawed without looking up.

The boy finished his fish and wiped his mouth on his sleeve.

'You like sprats then?'

'Never had them before. Never had anything like that.'

The boy looked surprised.

'So. What kind of a name is *Moss*?'

She'd never really thought about it. 'Dunno.' She sucked on a sprat bone. 'What's *your* name?'

'Salter.'

'Salter? That's a *name*?'

'I don't think yer in much of a position to slag it off.'

152

Moss grinned and saw a flicker at the corner of the boy's mouth.

'It's on account of me sleepin in a salt box when I was a babe. No money for a cradle, see. Bet yer used to tuckin up in a nice warm pallet, eh?'

'Well, yes, I suppose.' She thought of her bed, her blanket, the fire always lit. Things she'd always taken for granted. 'Have you always lived here then?'

'No,' said the boy, 'not always. Used to have a better place. Up Broken Wharf. You?'

'Oh, well, I . . . live in the forge.' Moss's stomach lurched as she thought of Pa. Probably out of his mind with worry. Quickly, she pushed the thought away. 'I mean I *used* to live in a forge. I'm on my way to . . . to my pa's sister. She lives in a village. She's going to get me work,' she added.

The boy raised his eyebrows, but said nothing.

'I can light fires. I can fetch and carry. She'll find me work in the village.'

'Is that right?' The boy wasn't looking, yet she felt like he saw straight through her. 'An' you just

153

come from the forge with nothin but the clothes on yer back?'

'Well, yes.'

'Got any money?'

Moss shook her head.

'How you gettin to yer auntie's?'

'I'll walk.'

'Know the way then?'

'Oh yes. Up the river a bit . . . through the city . . .'

Salter spat out a bitter chuckle. 'Girl like you, up in that city, they'll have yer boots *and* yer teeth before you've gone two streets!'

'Oh. I knew that. I'll mostly stick to the river.'

The wind whipped the flames of the fire and Moss drew her hands inside the sleeves of her dress. She gazed at the boy, at his fire, at his smoker and his shack and his boat. It occurred to her now that if she was going to last two days outside the Tower she'd need more than a pair of boots and a pocketful of crumbs. She needed to learn where to find food, how to make a shelter, things she'd never had to do for herself before. And here was a boy, living by the river, looking after himself. Maybe he could help her find the mill?

Down on the water's edge, a handful of children were playing, skimming pebbles across the waves. A woman came out of one of the huts, and when she noticed the children, her cry made Moss jump.

'Get away from that water!' she shrieked. 'If I've told you once, I've told you a thousand times! Devil knows what's waitin to crawl out of that river! Now get inside and don't come out till I tell yer!'

The children ran back up the shore, getting a cuff on the ears as they were bustled inside the hut.

'What was all that about?' asked Moss.

'River's a dangerous place. Kids forget that,' he said. 'I'm goin up Belinsgate later. To sell me sprats.'

'Belinsgate?'

'The fish market. You ain't never been there?'

'Oh. Well, Pa's very busy . . . we don't get out much.'

'Come with me, if yer like.' He flicked a fish

bone into the fire. 'Or not. Suit yerself.'

Moss hesitated. There was something about this boy. He was rude and sullen and seemed almost perpetually angry about one thing or another. And yet he'd shared his food with a stranger. Given her back her boots. Perhaps he wasn't all bad.

'Thank you,' said Moss. 'I'll come to Belinsgate.'

But a voice whispered in her ear.

Don't forget, this boy is a thief.

Salter's little boat bobbed over the waves. He'd dragged it into the river as soon as they'd finished breakfast, shrugging off Moss's offer of help. She could see that the boat weighed hardly anything at all and she'd wondered whether the rough water wouldn't just smash it to pieces.

Now she clung to its sides as Salter rowed upriver with deft strokes.

'Settle yerself, shore girl, she ain't about to tip. Made her meself.'

'You did? How?'

'Bit of this, bit of that I find on the shore. Stuff washed up, dropped from ships, wreck-wood that comes in with the tide.' He grinned. 'One man's rubbish is another man's gold.'

Through the dawn mist, Moss could make out the soaring arches of London Bridge. On the banks, close to where the boat now bobbed, was a sprinkling of sheds and booths. A line of women trickled from the city carrying baskets on their backs, warming the air with their chatter.

'Fisherwives. Catch is comin in,' said Salter.

He beached the little boat on the shore and hopped out. Moss followed him up the wide steps of Belinsgate Wharf.

All along the gangways sticking out from the wharf, men were jumping out of ships, rolling barrels and humping crates of fish, tipping them on to the banks where they lay like heaps of silver coin waiting for the wives to sort them into baskets. The shore was a market, heaving with people and animals.

Costermongers cursed their donkeys, sliding on the ice-hard mud, and barrow boys tugged handcarts laden with pitted piles of shrimps.

The air was bone-snapping raw. The talk was of fish and the cold. Men who made it their business to know the tides and the weather shook their heads.

'Freeze is comin,' said one. 'Been a long time since we had a winter like this.'

'So long as she don't ice up,' said another. 'Put us all out of business.' There were murmurs of agreement from the fisherwives.

The chatter broke off as an eerie creaking echoed across the river. Everyone on the wharf stopped what they were doing, trying to work out where the noise was coming from. The creak became a groan, filling the air, like the cry of some great felled beast.

From the direction of London Bridge came screams. Moss whipped round. She heard the sound of cracking stone and the rip of splintering wood, and looked up just in time to see a chunk of arch crumbling into the water, dragging with it a large wooden hut. From bobbing boats up and down the river, the watermen were shouting.

'The privy! She's gone in!'

'Men under! Men under the bridge!'

Salter was already running down to the shore. Moss sprinted after him. In the fast-flowing river she saw several men floundering. Their cries were tiny. People were leaning over the bridge, pointing and shouting. Salter was in the shallows now, dragging his boat off the shingle.

'Wait!' yelled Moss. If she hesitated, it was only for a moment. Before Salter could protest she was scrambling in after him.

'Sit down!' he panted, pushing and heaving on the oars as he fought to keep control of the little boat. 'Don't move unless I says so. If the boat tips, I'll deal with it.' They locked eyes briefly.

'Ain't got no chance,' he muttered, yet he was hauling on his oars with a strength that surprised Moss.

She could hear the roar of the drop on the other

side of the bridge. It was deafening. Like a waterfall. In the flimsy boat she felt the river surging forward, as if angry to find its progress blocked by the wide feet of the arches driven deep into its bed. If they got too close, they'd be sucked through.

'There's one!' she cried. A man, pinned by the current against the base of an arch, was clinging to the stonework with one hand. The other hand batted the water, a feeble fight against the river that was ripping at his body.

Now the boat was picking up speed. 'Hang on!' bellowed Salter as they plunged towards the bridge. The current had them and Salter stood, feet astride, driving one oar deep into the water in an attempt to steer the boat nearer to the arches. Moss gripped the sides and screamed as the boat slammed into a wall of stone. The force of the collision catapulted her forward and her head took a blow from the seat.

'Get up!' yelled Salter, throwing the oars into the bottom of the boat. He lunged at the side of the stone arch.

Moss clawed her way forward on her hands and knees and when she came up, Salter was clinging to a rusty chain bolted into the foot of the arch.

'Hold this!' he cried, threading the mooring rope through the chain. He thrust the rope end into Moss's hands. 'Don't let it slip. Use yer legs to keep us close to the arch.' And before she could protest he was wobbling to the front of the boat with an oar in his hand. Moss scanned the river. Where was the man? She caught sight of an arm flailing beside the next arch. The force of the current was still pinning him to the stone.

They'd overshot. They'd gone an arch too far. And now she understood what Salter was trying to do.

'No!' she cried as he dropped into the water. With one arm hooked over the side, he reached with the other, extending the oar towards the man. The man stretched towards him, but it was no good. Salter was too far away.

'You'll have to let go!' cried Salter to the man, his words snatched by the white noise of the river.

'Push off with yer feet! Hard! Then grab me oar!'

The man stared with mad eyes. A wound on his head bled into the water. Moss doubted he could even move, let alone launch himself far enough to get hold of the oar.

'Now!' shouted Salter. The man hesitated, then heaved his body out into the surging current. In the split second before he was snatched away under the bridge, Salter loosened his armlock on the boat until he was clinging only by his fingertips, extending the reach of the oar by a couple of feet. The man swiped at it, missing with one hand, but somehow managing to wind his other arm round the end.

'You've got him!' yelled Moss. But she could see that Salter's grip on the boat was slipping. As quickly as her trembling hands would allow, she fastened the rope in a rough knot and threw herself across the boat, scrabbling to Salter's side, where she snatched his hand and dragged him back to grasp hold of the boat's side once more. The man clung to the end of the oar, his body thrashing from side to side in the current. Then strangely and suddenly, the grey river turned green. All around them was a tangle of riverweed.

Moss screamed. Something was pulling on her elbow. She looked down and saw a fist of riverweed tight round it. She tore at it with her free hand, but the weed had her snagged tight. Then she heard laughter, snatched by the roar of the river, and the weed went slack.

'The rope!' cried Salter.

Taut as a stick, the rope was juddering through the chain as Moss's knot unravelled. She stumbled back and fell on the end of the rope just as it was about to whip through the chain.

When she looked back at the river, the man had gone.

The riverweed melted away. And, though she couldn't be sure, for a split second she could have sworn she saw the head of a pale woman cut through the waves.

Chapter Fourteen
Bread First Then Morals

Moss and Salter had made their way back to his shack in silence.

Salter's face was storm-cloud angry and even though Moss was bursting with questions, she thought better of asking them.

She looked up from the fire she'd just started in Salter's pit. He was banging out a broken board on the boat, muttering and swearing.

'We tried to save him,' said Moss.

'Fat lot of good our tryin turned out to be

for the poor fella who's fish food now.'

'At least we tried.'

'Well, try this!' Salter was half yelling at her now. 'YOU are a crazy idiot. Jumpin in me boat like that! An' if you'd fallen in? What then? You can't even swim!'

Moss blinked. Was he angry at *her* now?

'I . . . I just wanted to help.'

'Well, next time save yer kindness.'

His voice softened a little. 'Down on the river, death ain't so far away. You blacksmiths' girls got no idea. An' I ain't just talkin about drownin.' He laid down the chipped hammer he was using and looked at Moss. 'There's children gone missin from the shore these past months. Not drowned. Not runaways. Just gone.'

'What do you mean, gone?' said Moss.

'I don't know. I ain't seen nothin. Snatched is what the fishermen say.'

Moss shivered a little, remembering what Nell had told her. 'What else do the fishermen say?'

Salter just shrugged.

The fire Moss had lit was chewing up the driftwood and she huddled close, fanning out her sodden dress until steam rose off the wool. She thought of the warm forge fire and for a moment glimpsed Pa, grey face creased with worry. Was he looking for her? He wouldn't have to go far. Salter's shack was just a short walk from the Tower. A surge of anger tightened her chest. All these years, pretending they were prisoners. *Liar.*

She looked up from the flames to find Salter watching her.

'You ain't got no auntie in a village, have you, Leatherboots?'

She shook her head.

'And you ain't got no place to go.'

'I do have somewhere to go,' said Moss. 'It's just that I don't know how to get there.'

'What's this place called then?'

'Hampton. Do you know it?'

Salter laughed. 'Hampton? What, Hampton

Court? Don't seem like quite the place fer you, even with yer leather boots.'

'Hampton . . . the Hampton Wheel, I think.'

Salter shrugged. 'Hampton's a long way from here. Maybe a day's row.'

The tightness in her chest vanished. 'Could you take me?'

'You gonna pay me?'

'You know I haven't got any money.'

Salter grinned. 'Better get you to work then.'

He peeled the broken board from his boat with a snap and kicked it into the fire. 'You can stay here a few days. Light the fire and smoke the sprats while I'm workin the river.'

Moss didn't know what to say. She was tired. She was wet. She could feel the cold creeping through her bones. This boy had food. He had shelter. And maybe he'd take her to Hampton. Maybe . . .

The warning voice whispered in her ear again.

Don't forget. He's a thief.

That evening they shared two of Salter's smoked sprats and he let her tuck herself into a corner of his shack. It was bigger than it looked from the outside. And to Moss's surprise, inside it was snug and warm. All right, so there was a little row of rats' tails nailed to the door, which Salter said were drying out for fish bait. But he'd made a fine job of sealing the roof with pine pitch to keep out the rain. The gaps in the walls were plugged with mud and straw, there was an upturned crate for a table, two simple stools made from driftwood, a straw pallet just like her own in the forge, and he'd even stuffed a small sack with feathers to make a pillow.

'I never felt anything so soft,' said Moss. 'Where did you get the feathers?'

'Traded em,' replied Salter gruffly.

'What, with your fish?'

'Nah.' He gave Moss a look. 'I trades the other stuff I gets.'

'Other stuff? You mean things you steal?'

'That's right.'

'You think it's all right to rob people?' she asked.

'Yep.' Salter rocked back on his stool. 'Don't you?'

'Of course not.'

'Yer daddy gives you everythin you need, does he? Clothes, boots, puts food on yer table. Well, it ain't like that fer me. Bread first then morals, Miss Leatherboots.'

Moss was quiet.

'But listen.' He broke into a sudden grin. 'When I ain't thievin or lyin, I is the most respectable boy you could meet!'

Moss tried not to smile. 'So you live all alone then?'

'Yep.'

'No mother or father?'

'Gone. One night Mum come down with the fever and she was dead by mornin.'

'Oh, I'm sorry.'

'Sorry don't cover it.'

'And your father?'

'Dad was a waterman. Knew the old Thames better than anyone on the North Bank.' He stopped.

Moss hesitated. 'So what happened?'

'Bunch of lords on the lash,' said Salter bitterly. 'Off their heads on mead. Wanted to shoot the bridge, didn't they?'

'Shoot the bridge?'

'London Bridge. At full tide there's a ten-foot drop over the other side. Black Suck we calls it. It'll pull you over and drag you down, quick as a pike with a frog. They wanted Dad to ride the water through the bridge. Guess they must have paid him well enough. Anyway, he did it. Boat turned over. Passin barge pulled out the lords but, I dunno, I guess they didn't see Dad.'

'He drowned?'

'He drowned. Ain't a day goes by when I don't think about me dad and me mum.'

'Salter?'

'Yes?'

'What did you see today? In the river.'

Salter eyed her. 'What d'you mean?'

'The riverweed that came up so suddenly. I

thought I saw . . . I don't know . . . a head,' said Moss. 'Did you see it?'

'Nope,' said Salter a little too quickly.

'But –'

'But nothin. You see a lot of things out on that river. Water plays tricks on yer eyes.'

They stopped talking then and the hut was quiet save for the lapping of the waves on the shingle outside. A melody drifted into her head and before she really knew what she was doing, Moss found herself singing the haunting words Nell had sung to her back in the forge, the night Pa had flown into such a rage.

> *Silver river stained with souls*
> *Take care of its depths, my child*
> *When frost and ice creep from her shores*
> *She'll drag you down, my child*
>
> *A miller's daughter once she was*
> *Spurned on her wedding day*

She seeks the thing she'll never have
A loving child to hold

Moss looked over at Salter. His eyes were closed.

She is the waves, the current strong
The weed that snags your feet
And if she finds you, better drown
Than feel her cold embrace

'Been a long time since I heard that.' Salter opened his eyes and hugged his knees to his chest. 'The song of the river. Me mum used to sing it to send me off to sleep.'

'Salter?'

'Mmmm.'

'The Riverwitch . . . do you believe in her?'

'It's just a song. To scare the young'uns.'

'But you've seen strange things on the river,' Moss persisted. 'Have you ever seen something that might be her? Do you know anyone who has?'

'You don't give up easy, do yer?' Salter rubbed his dirt-smudged face. 'All I know is them that works the river keeps their children away from the water in winter. And that if a child falls in, they hopes it drowns quick before the Riverwitch can get to it.'

'Why?' asked Moss.

Salter spat on his hand and crossed himself.

'The fishermen say, that if she finds a child, she'll take it, drag it down deep. That she'll suck the warmth from its heart, and its body will be lost to the river forever. But they're just stories an' if I want to make a livin, I can't afford to believe in them.'

'And the snatcher? The one taking the children from the shore? Do you think that's the Riverwitch?'

Salter shrugged. 'Like I said, it ain't no feast day down here. If yer livin on the river, shore girl, better keep yer wits handy.'

'So if –'

'Right,' said Salter abruptly, 'I'm goin' to sleep now. If you know what's good, you'll do the same.'

'But –'

'Ain't never known a freeze like this. Colder than a dead dog in snow.' He threw her a sack. 'Sleep tight.' Salter rolled himself up and was gently snoring before Moss had even got her boots off.

Moss lay awake, her head buzzing with what she'd seen on the river that day. The weed that had snagged her arm. The face. Had she really seen it? Or was it the water playing tricks, like Salter said?

She listened to the waves lapping in and out on the shingle, a rhythm like the breath of sleep. It was strange. She'd lived her whole life by this river, but behind the Tower walls she'd never really heard its sounds before.

Realising she was still wide awake, Moss sat up. As softly as she could, she pulled on her boots and crept out into the cold. A patch of wet prickled the end of her nose. She looked up. The moon on the river lit up a blurry white sky. Moss stuck out her tongue, tasting the clean fizz of melting snowflakes.

The river was beautiful in the milky light. Moss could just about make out the blunt turrets of the

Tower, faint as an old tapestry through the falling flakes. Her eyes followed the line of the river and something caught her attention halfway between the Tower and where she now stood. An orange flame was flickering. She peered through the flakes. It seemed to be coming from a lantern, creaking this way and that.

The night was very still under the falling snow. The lantern licked its way up the shore, towards a small collection of tumbledown huts close to the edge of the river. One by one it sought them out, fingers of light poking into their darkest corners. Moss stared, hypnotised by its progress. As it came closer, she could see the figure who was carrying it. A man, his back bent, his frayed cloak a silhouette against the moonlit river. Moss's breath caught in her throat.

The ragged man.

Quickly, Moss leapt back inside the shack, slammed the door shut and pressed herself against it. Salter shot bolt upright.

'What?!'

'Nothing,' she replied. 'Nothing really. I'm sorry I woke you.'

But Moss felt the dread crawl down her spine like a worm.

The ragged man. What was he doing, wandering the shore with a lantern?

Looking for something?

Or looking for *someone*?

CHAPTER FIFTEEN
Frost Fair

Moss had never seen it snow like this. It fell, day after day, thick as pudding, until every dirty street was layered with white. It was cold too. Colder than she'd ever known. And all the while, the river was changing. The fast flow of water slowed to a crawl. Then one morning, a week after that first night in Salter's shack, Moss woke up to find the River Thames had frozen solid.

She worked as hard as she could for Salter. She lit his fire, she gathered driftwood and tinder. She learnt how the smoker worked and she mended his net. She wondered how long it would be before Salter rowed her to Hampton. A few days he'd said, but now the river was frozen she'd just have to wait. In some ways she didn't mind at all. There was something about this boy thief that intrigued her. She didn't like him exactly. How could she? He'd pulled her out of the river, not from the goodness of his heart, but to steal her boots. He'd given them back though. Given her a roof and food, and she had no idea why. Because he felt sorry for her? Because he wanted someone to fetch and carry for him? One good thing though – he didn't ask many questions. And for that she was thankful.

That morning, Moss had woken to a hoar frost. Rooftops twinkled silver-purple. Icicles crackled in the winter sun. Children ran out from doorways to roll in the fine powder. Chestnut sellers appeared on every corner and there was a quiet like Moss had never known.

She stood on the shore. A crowd had gathered,

watching as forty watermen linked arms to walk across the ice. When they reached the other side there was a huge cheer and everyone ran on to the river. Moss stuck to the shallows, thumping it with her foot. It creaked but didn't break. She skidded her way down to the bridge where hunks of frozen river clogged beneath the arches. She wouldn't have believed it possible. An unstoppable torrent just days before, now the river was as still as rock.

Moss stepped on to the ice and touched the rough stone. Then she looked back at the shore, stretching all the way past Belinsgate Wharf to the Tower. If she squinted, she could just make out Salter's shack, beyond the fishermen's huts.

Her eye snapped back to the huts. A lone figure was walking up the shore, broad and round-shouldered like a bear. Every now and then he'd stop to talk to the people he passed. And when he'd finished, he'd turn away and trudge on up the shingle, his shoulders drooping and heavy.

It was Pa.

He was looking for her.

Moss found herself backing round the arch. Watching him. He was quite close now, walking towards the edge of the frozen river. As he stared blankly across the ice, she saw sunken eyes in an ash-white face, etched with the worry and pain that she'd seen that last evening in the forge.

She supposed she should feel sorry for him, but she didn't. Instead, rage swelled her chest until she wanted to cry out every one of Salter's foul-mouthed curses at her father for his lies. The Executioner. The man who would trade freedom for meat on the table and a roof over his head. He'd chosen his life. Well, it didn't have to be *hers*.

Pa turned from the river and began walking slowly up the bank towards the city. Twice he slipped on the frozen mud. She watched his huge body fall. Heard the thud of his shoulder as it hit the ground. It must have hurt, but he did not cry out. Just picked himself up and staggered on.

Moss backed further round the arch, fighting

the urge to call out to him. She did not want
to be found.

By the time she returned to the shack, Salter was
squatting by the fire, stirring a pot of foul-smelling
liquid. His upturned boat was next to him and two
slender pieces of driftwood lay in the snow.

'What are you doing?'

'Waterman still needs to make a livin, even when
there ain't no water. In this city it's everyone fer
himself.'

He dragged his upturned boat closer to the fire.

'Goin to turn me boat into a sled. You can help
me.' He pointed to the bubbling pot. 'Keep stirrin'
and don't let it boil.'

'What is it?' said Moss, trying not to wrinkle
her nose.

'Fish glue.'

'Really? You can make glue?'

'Yep. Fish skins and water. Bonds tight as a limpet

on a rock and it don't cost nothin. I ain't got money to waste on glue and tools.' He began hacking off the rough edges of the driftwood with a knife.

'Where do you get your tools then?'

'Washed up on the shore. Or I makes em meself.'

Moss looked around at Salter's motley collection of instruments. A hammer with the end chipped off, a handful of twisted iron nails, a knife bound with twine at the handle where the wood must have worn away.

'Guess this ain't what yer used to, bein a blacksmith's girl? Must be fine tools all over the place. Reckon you got a nice life, all cosy in yer dad's warm forge.'

Moss hesitated. What harm could it do to tell Salter a little more about herself? Maybe he'd understand why she'd run away.

'My pa is a blacksmith. He works in the Tower of London. But . . .' She took a deep breath. 'He's also the King's Executioner.'

'So?'

'Well, I've lived in the Tower for as long as I can remember. Until I found this tunnel and, well, I escaped.'

'*Escaped?*'

'We were prisoners.'

'In the Tower of London? What, are you royalty or somethin?' Salter chuckled.

'No, Pa . . . Pa pretended . . . well, we weren't really prisoners . . . well, he did something . . .' As Moss struggled to find the words, she realised she could barely figure it all out herself, never mind retell it. And this boy thief was practically a stranger.

'Pa does all the Tower beheadings. I help him. He chops off the heads, I scoop them up in a basket.'

Salter raised an eyebrow. 'Well, ain't you a shadowy little cat? Takes some guts to do that, I should think.'

Moss shrugged.

'An' I had you pinned as a spoilt little blacksmith's girl. Used to a warm hearth and a nice supper. But there's more to you, ain't there, Leatherboots?'

He carried on scraping. Through the dirt on his face she could feel him studying her from the corner of his eye. Trying to work her out. She wouldn't tell him any more. Not just yet.

'Still, bet yer dad makes a coin or two up on that scaffold. I heard the prisoner always gives the Executioner money to make em die quick.'

'Blood money,' said Moss.

'Money is money,' said Salter.

'Not for me.'

'Spoken like a girl who ain't never felt the hunger eatin her from the inside out. Who ain't never been afraid. Who ain't wanted for nothin.'

'There are plenty of things I want,' protested Moss. 'And I'll tell you something. None of them are inside that Tower.'

'An' you think they're out here? In this city where yer throat'll be cut fer a loaf of bread?'

Moss had no answer to that. Salter could say what he liked. *He* didn't have a father who'd locked him in a tower and lied to him his whole life.

Salter stopped scraping and put down his knife, and for a moment his expression seemed almost tender through the dirt-smudge of his face.

'Sometimes you don't know what you got, till you ain't got it no more.'

Eventually the boat-sled was ready and Salter insisted they try it out, even though it was already dark. They dragged it down to the river's edge. So absorbed had Moss been in the making of the sled that when they got there her eyes gaped wide. Lacing the crystal ice was the criss-cross glow of a thousand burning torches.

'Frost Fair!' cried Salter.

Moss had never seen anything like it. The frozen river was alive with people. Harlequin tents flapped in the night breeze, the warm smell of spiced beer drifted up the bank and a line of archers pulled back their bows, sending a flock of flaming arrows thudding into their targets. On the Southwark side,

185

a ring of hay bales penned a bear that snorted and shook the ring in its nose while its owner beat time on a drum. And everywhere people were skating and sliding, giggling as they toppled in heaps. The river was a river no more. Sleeping like a giant, thought Moss, while all of London danced on its back.

Salter was sitting on the bank, stuffing extra straw into his shoes.

'Wrap up warm,' he said and launched himself on to the ice, wobbling a little way out, trying to push his feet forward. It wasn't long before he was slipping and sliding across the frozen river.

'You might want a bit of practice before you take on paying customers!' called Moss.

'Yep, that's what *you* is here for, Leatherboots!' he said with a grin. 'Throw me the rope!'

Moss picked up the rope attached to the boat-sled and threw it out on to the ice.

'Now give it a shove and jump in!'

She did as she was told, more out of curiosity than anything.

186

Salter hoisted the rope over his shoulder and pulled. In a surprisingly short time he'd got the hang of it and was zigzagging across the river with Moss in tow. She wrapped a piece of sacking round herself and leant out, watching the ice rush by.

So much had changed. It felt almost unreal. She was on a sled. Pulled by a boy who made a living rowing people across the river and stealing from them. Staying in his shack. Eating his food. Strangely, enjoying his company. But best of all, she was free. She could stay. She could leave. There was no one to tell her what to do. No heads to scoop up in a basket. No walls. No Pa.

Moss looked down as they rushed over the ice. A shadow was moving with them, close to the sled. Moss blinked several times, thinking it must be the play of torchlight. But as she looked closer, she could see that it wasn't. It was under the ice. Moving slowly. Lazily. A green-black shadow. Then it was gone.

'Hey!' called Salter. 'Over there, look!' He steered towards the middle of the ice where a huge blaze was burning. 'You hungry?'

'Starving,' said Moss.

'Me too,' said Salter. 'An' there's a farthin burnin a hole in me pocket.'

Slowing the sled, he waited while Moss clambered out. She followed him, slipping and skidding to where the fire was roaring into the night sky. On one side, men had raked aside hot logs and were roasting a pig. People were gathered round, laughing as the fire spat greasy sparks into the night sky.

'Won't it melt the ice?'

'Nope. It's too thick now.'

Salter led her round the stalls that clustered near the roasting pig, sniffing at the piles of hot gingerbreads, grinning at the wafting scent of clove-spiced ale and stopping eventually in front of a stall stacked high with pies.

'Mutton-raisin pies!' a man hollered and held out the golden-skinned pies to the gathering crowds. 'Threefarthin! Mutton-raisin pies! Only threefarthin!

'Ahh,' groaned Salter, 'ain't nothin so good as a mutton-raisin pie.' He dug in his pockets, fished out a coin, frowned and walked up to the pieman.

'Smells good, mate,' said Salter.

'Threefarthin,' said the man, eyeing him.

'I'll have one then,' said Salter.

The pieman handed over a pie. As Salter took it, he fumbled it, nearly dropped it, but managed to hold on, scrunching it back together.

'Give us yer money then,' said the pieman.

'Hang on a minute,' said Salter. 'What's this?' He lifted the pastry lid of his pie and pulled out what looked to Moss very much like a rat's tail.

'Saints' armpits!' he cried, thrusting the tail in the pieman's face. 'You cheatin thief! Bulking out with rats' tails and devil knows what else!'

'What are you talkin about?' said the pieman, 'I ain't cheatin nobody!'

'Then what do you call *this?*' said Salter,

waggling the tail in front of his nose.

'Those filthy pockets of yours are full of tails for all I know,' growled the pieman.

By now a few people in the crowd were turning to see what the commotion was.

'People are lookin,' said Salter. 'That can't be good for business.'

The pieman glanced around. 'There's no problem here,' he piped.

'That's right,' said Salter to the seller in a low voice. 'Now, mate, tell you what. I'll give you a farthin for the pie. Keep the tail. An' we'll say no more.'

'Why, you little –' hissed the pieman. He looked nervously at the crowd, who were beginning to point at the tail Salter held aloft.

The pieman snatched the tail and the farthing and thrust them in his pocket with a scowl. 'Now get on out of it, yer little runt!'

Salter grinned and hustled Moss out of the crowd.

Back at the sled he divided the pie in two and handed a piece to Moss.

'Ahh, God,' said Salter, devouring his piece as though it might get up and run away if he didn't eat it quick enough. 'What's the matter? You not hungry now?'

'What just happened there?' said Moss.

'What you talkin about?' said Salter, eyes wide as moons.

'You *know* what,' said Moss. 'The rat's tail!' The warm pie in her hand smelt very good.

'Go on,' said Salter, 'it fair melts in yer mouth.'

Moss nibbled a bit off the end. It tasted every bit as delicious as it smelt. Ravenous, she crammed the rest into her mouth, suspicions forgotten.

'Thanks,' she said, her mouth stuffed with juicy raisins and mutton.

'Don't mention it,' said Salter. His eyes crinkled in the orange torchlight. 'Tomorrow we'll make some money.'

'On your boat-sled?'

He grinned. 'There's more than one way to make a livin on the river.'

CHAPTER SIXTEEN
Salter's Scam

One thing Moss could say about her new life – it wasn't easy. Freeze or no freeze, everybody on the river rose at the crack of dawn. As soon as the first rays of sun peeped over the water, the shore was buzzing.

Salter had hurried off with several strings of smoked sprats. To Eastcheap market, he'd said, where he'd get a good price the earlier he went.

Salter was a constant puzzle to Moss. She couldn't understand how he'd save a person's life one minute and rob them blind the next. He shared his food and shelter with her – a person he barely knew and whom he clearly didn't think much of.

Yet there was also an openness about Salter and she liked that. She liked that he didn't pretend.

When she'd laid the fire she wandered down to the water's edge and found herself walking in the direction of the Tower. The river was still crammed with people eating, selling, laughing and shouting. It was almost as rowdy as Tower Hill on Execution Day, but the atmosphere was different somehow. There was no hunger about this crowd. They hadn't come for blood. They'd come to play. And it struck Moss what a twisted view of the world she'd had from inside the Tower, with its executions, baying crowds, spiked heads –

'Ow!'

Her foot struck something hard. She looked down and what she saw made her laugh out loud. Sticking up out of the ice was the handle of an axe. She'd know that axe anywhere. It was Pa's. Frozen in the shallows of the river. It must have washed to shore, then got stuck as the retreating river froze solid.

Gripping the handle, Moss pulled and jiggled and kicked it with her foot until she'd worked it loose enough to yank it from the ice. It lay cold and heavy in her hands. The wide blade Pa had kept so bright was dull and grey. He would barely recognise it now.

Moss wondered what to do with it. Its days on the hill were done. Maybe she could use it to chop driftwood for the fire? But the thought of chopping anything with that axe turned her stomach. Still, she'd seen how Salter scavenged for every scrap of iron on the shore. Perhaps he could make use of it somehow?

By the time she got back to the shack, dusk was falling. She dug a shallow hole in the shingle nearby, buried the axe in it and threw a pile of sacks on top.

'Oi, Oi!'

Moss looked up at the cry and Salter's head

poked round the side of the hut. He was carrying a flat, open box covered in a piece of cloth.

'You been good while I was gone?' he said, and before she could reply he thrust the box under her nose. The warm smell of freshly cooked pastry wafted from under the cloth. They hadn't eaten yet that day and Moss was starving. Salter grinned, looking mighty pleased with himself.

'Take a look,' he said and pulled back the cloth to reveal a boxful of apple tarts, crisp layers of pastry weeping buttery juice. 'Taffety tarts,' said Salter.

'You sold all your sprats to buy *these*?'

'Yep. These tarts are goin to make us some money.'

He thrust the box into Moss's hands and grabbed two large crates.

'Come on, shore girl, we're goin on the river.'

'Don't we get to eat one first?'

'Nah, they're not fer us to eat.'

'We're going to sell them?'

'Somethin like that.'

It was dark by the time Salter had chosen his spot on the river. He plonked down the crates and placed the box of tarts on top of one. Once again, the ice was lit by the glow of torches and Moss warmed to the sound of chatter and laughter.

'Take these,' said Salter. He pressed two coins into Moss's hand. She turned them over. Two pennies.

'Why?' said Moss. 'What do you want me to do with them?'

'I'm goin to be sellin these taffetys,' said Salter, 'an' yer goin to help me. All you got to do is use the pennies to buy the first one. Eat it then leave. I'll meet you under the middle arch of the Bridge.'

'But you could buy two loaves of bread with this,' said Moss. 'No one in their right mind would pay twopence for a tart!'

Salter shot her a crafty look. 'Leave the details to me, Leatherboots. Now you go and mingle with the crowd and when I start sellin, don't you forget, yer the first to buy. Got it?'

'All right,' said Moss. He was up to something, she

knew it. But selling tarts seemed harmless enough. And even if she was the only one to pay twopence, it was his money anyway. She wriggled into the crowd and watched Salter climb on to a crate.

'Ladies and gents!' he yelled. 'Gather round, gather round! Who's feelin the pinch of cold?'

No one really seemed to be looking his way.

'The bite of a hard winter?'

The crowds were passing. They glanced up at him and at the covered box on the other crate, but they all walked by.

'Ladies and gents! Who is up fer makin some *money!*'

Now *that* caught the attention of a few.

'Lucky, lucky! Are you feelin lucky?' he shouted. He dug in his pockets and pulled out something round and bright in each hand.

'Two gold crowns!' Salter held the crowns aloft and a murmur rippled through the crowd that was now growing around him.

Two gold crowns! Where had he got that kind

of money, Moss wondered. Not from selling sprats, that was for sure. Two gold crowns were a month's wages for the Stableman back in the Tower.

Now the crowd was beginning to buzz.

'Gather round, gather round an' watch,' said Salter. 'Watch carefully, ladies and gents.' He bent down and whisked off the cloth from the box. The smell of the taffetys wafted into the night air. 'Fresh taffetys, lovely as you like!' he said. 'Who ain't lickin their lips now? But I ain't sellin tarts. I'm sellin the chance to make a small fortune today, ladies and gents.'

He waved the gold crowns in the air. Then he picked up a tart and popped a crown inside, squeezing the hole tight so it wouldn't fall out. He did the same with the other crown in another tart. Then he placed the tarts back in the tray and switched them all around. The crowd peered in. No one could tell which tarts had the crowns in and which were just tarts.

'Now then! Your chance to win a gold crown! Ten

tarts! Two crowns! If I was the bettin type I'd say that was good odds! What will you give me, ladies and gents, fer the chance to win a crown? Who wants first pick? What'll you give? Who's in for a shillin?'

'You must be jokin!' called out someone in the crowd.

'All right then,' said Salter, 'sixpence! Who'll give me sixpence?' The crowd was silent. 'All right, drown me in the river if I ain't offerin charity at threepence a tart! No one? Twopence then!'

Twopence . . . Moss was so mesmerised by Salter's easy patter that she almost forgot her cue. Twopence!

'Me,' she croaked. 'Me! Twopence! I'll buy one of your tarts.'

'Did I hear twopence at the back there?' cried Salter.

Moss pushed her way to the front and held out her two pennies.

'One young lady, two pennies it is!' said Salter and gestured to the box. 'Choose a tart an' may luck be yer friend!'

199

Moss wasn't quite sure what to do next. All he'd said was that she should buy a tart. She handed over the pennies. Which one should she choose?

'Come on, come on! There's people here wantin a turn before they're too old to smell their own farts! Let's have yer choice and let's have it quick!' Salter shook the box.

'That one,' said Moss, pointing to a tart in the middle.

'Right you are, young lady,' said Salter. He picked up the tart. She saw something glint between his fingers, then it was gone. *Was it a coin?* Had he kept one back and just stuffed it in the tart? She *knew* he was up to something.

'Take a bite then, miss,' said Salter. 'Everyone wants to know if yer a winner.'

Moss bit into the tart and as the pastry crumbled down her chin, her teeth chomped on something hard. She extracted the tart from her mouth and a gold crown dropped into her hand.

'Oooooh!' went the crowd.

'Well, that's what I call lucky!' cried Salter. 'Off you go, young lady, an' don't spend it all at once! Now who else is feelin the tinglin touch of Lady Luck? Who's next at twopence a time?!'

The crowd closed in, all shouting and waving pennies at Salter. One by one they handed over their money, bit into their tarts and were disappointed. Soon there were just two tarts in the box.

'Two taffetys left!' cried Salter. 'And one of them has the crown. Last chance! What am I bid for a fifty-fifty chance of winnin a gold crown? Who'll start me at a shillin?'

Moss gasped. A shilling! That was more than most of these people probably earned in a day.

'One shilling!' called out a rough-throated man.

'One shilling, twopence!' called out someone else.

'One shilling and fourpence!'

'Any advance on one shillin an' fourpence?!' cried Salter. 'Fifty-fifty chance of winnin a gold crown, ladies and gents!'

A few people looked like they couldn't make up their minds.

'Come on, don't be shy!' cried Salter.

'One shilling and sixpence!' called someone.

'Any advance on one shillin an' sixpence!' yelled Salter. 'Last chance at one shillin an' sixpence. Goin once! Goin twice! Gone to the lady in brown! Come on up, missus, an' try yer luck!'

A woman hurried to the front. Her dress was well worn and she didn't look like she could afford a shilling and sixpence, thought Moss. But maybe she'd be lucky. A gold crown would be worth it. Why shouldn't she try her luck?

The woman handed her money to Salter, who held out the box. She hesitated, staring at the two tarts, and tried not to look at the gawping crowd. Then she reached for one and broke it open with her hands.

'Ahhhhh,' went the crowd.

The woman bit her lip and Moss could tell she was trying not to cry. Dropping the broken tart to the ground she pushed her way back through the crowd.

'What am I bid for the last of the taffetys, ladies and gents!' cried Salter. 'I said I'd sell them all and I'll keep me word!'

'A shilling sixpence!' called someone.

'A shilling and eight!'

'A shilling and ten!'

Two shillings!'

'Ooooh!' gasped the crowd.

'Two shillings!' yelled Salter. 'Any advance on two shillings? No? Going once! Twice! Sold to the gent on me left. Come on up, sir, and take yer prize!'

The man stepped forward and handed Salter the two shillings. Salter offered him the box and he took the last taffety tart. There was not a whisper in the crowd as they waited to see him break open the tart and claim his gold crown. The man bit into the taffety. *Chomp, chomp* went his teeth. He bit again. He was chewing. A frown spread over his face. As he broke open the rest of the tart and crumbled it to the floor, Salter tossed the box into the air, sprang from his upturned crate and dived into the crowd.

'THIEF!' roared the man. 'There ain't no gold crown in here! Come back, you son-of-a-poleaxe! I'll grind yer kneecaps to dust! GRAB HIM, SOMEONE!'

There was a huge commotion as people tried to catch the boy darting in and out of the crowd. Clumsy hands clutched thin air, bodies toppled over one another in the chaos, but Salter was too quick for them. And then he was gone.

Moss bent her head and backed out of the scrambling crowd as inconspicuously as she could. She knew what Salter had done and she was furious. When she caught up with him, she'd tell him exactly what she thought of him.

She started to make her way to London Bridge, but as she slipped in and out through the stalls, past the spit-roast fires, a hush swept down the ice. The crowd was parting. In front of her, people were dropping to their knees.

A silver sleigh was gliding up the ice towards them, pulled by a pair of beautiful greys. The horses trotted crisply, their coats rippling under a harness of tinkling bells. In the back was a mountain of white fur. It covered a man and, opposite him, a woman. All activity on the ice had stopped and the air sparked with awed whispers.

The King!

King Henry. Look!

The King and Queen ride by!

Through the haze of torchlight, Moss could make out the King's face, broad and red, a ginger beard sprouting just above his bull-thick neck. Wrapped round his mighty shoulders was a velvet cloak trimmed with ermine. He lay back against the seat of the sleigh with the satisfied look of someone who had just won a quarrel. Moss craned to see the Queen, but her neck was bent, her face hidden from view. Then, as the sleigh swept past, Queen Anne Boleyn lifted her head, staring over the ice with eyes that went beyond the crowd.

Moss couldn't tear her gaze from the Queen, remembering the cold words of that stone-eyed uncle. *Nothing can save her now.* Save her from what? The sleigh swept on up the river. And Moss could see that though she was wrapped in furs, though she rode a silver sleigh and sat next to a king, this Queen was troubled.

She looked utterly alone.

Under London Bridge, Moss found Salter, waiting.

'Come on, Leatherboots! Was you followed?'

Before she could reply, he yanked her arm and hustled her away from the bridge. But as they scrambled for the bank, a log in a nearby brazier popped so loudly it toppled the brazier to the ground, sending a shower of sparks shooting all around them.

'THERE HE IS!'

A group of men on the river pointed to Salter.

'Run, shore girl! This way!' Salter grabbed her

hand, pulled her into a narrow street and they ran.

'COME BACK HERE, YER LITTLE DEVIL! I'LL BREAK THOSE HANDS AND GRIND YER KNUCKLES TO DUST!'

Moss had never run so fast. Although it was Salter they were after, she didn't doubt that they would have her too if they were caught. After all, she had eaten the first tart and taken the first gold crown. They would think she was part of the trick, for sure. But the cries of the man grew fainter as they darted through the twisted streets. Moss's feet pounded the snow. Past alehouses they ran, past stalls packing up for the day, past shuttered shops.

'Come on!' panted Salter. He was grinning. 'Up Farringdon Hill.'

They heaved and panted up the hill through the heavy snow. When they reached the top, Salter stopped. Moss yanked her hand from his and fell on her knees, coughing into the freezing air. Salter reached in his pocket and pulled out a fistful of coins.

'One shillin . . . two shillins . . . three shillins . . .

four shillins and four pence . . . four shillins and six
. . . four shillins an' eight pence! That's one shillin
to Eel-Eye Jack fer the loan of the crowns. Three
shillins an' eightpence fer me! Not bad fer a day's
work, eh? Here.' He held out a shilling for Moss to
take. 'Take it, Leatherboots. Couldn't have done it
without yer.'

'I don't want your stinking money!' cried Moss
and batted it out of his hand. 'You robbed those
people!' She pulled the gold crown out of her
pocket and flung it down with the rest. 'There *was*
no crown in that last tart.'

'So?'

'So you as good as took their money from out of
their pockets. What you did was *wrong*, Salter!'

'Right an' wrong is for rich people. When you
gonna learn that, Leatherboots?'

'Never!' said Moss. She could feel the anger
burning a hole in her throat. He had *used* her.

'What, you never taken nothin?' said Salter. 'You
never snatched a scrap from anyone's table?'

'Only leftovers,' said Moss. 'It's hardly the same.'

'Look, Miss High-and-Mighty, the point is, when yer hungry, you do what you have to do.'

Moss shook her head. 'I don't do what you do. I don't scam people. I don't lie to them, deceive them, raise their hopes, steal from them.'

'If they're stupid or greedy enough to think they can get somethin fer nothin –'

'You stole their money, Salter. And you used *me* to do it. Is this why you said I could stay in your shack? Eat your food? So you could use me in your cheating tricks?'

'No.'

'*Yes*. It was. You were never going to take me up the river, were you? You're just a scammer. A thief. A *dirty thief*!'

Her words hung in the crisp air.

Salter looked at her and the crinkle went out of his eyes. She expected him to come back with something. More excuses. But he was silent.

If she'd hurt his feelings, she didn't care. He

was a dirty thief. And caught up in his scams and schemes, it made her feel dirty too.

'Look,' she said, 'you helped me. You gave me food and a roof. But cheating and stealing – it's not for me. I don't want to live that way. It's better if . . . if I don't stay any more.'

Salter's face set hard. 'Then be on yer way then.'

'Don't worry, I'm going.' Moss kicked the silver coin that lay in the snow. 'And you can keep your shilling,' she said.

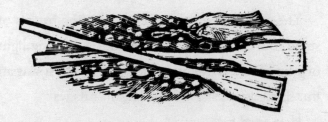

CHAPTER SEVENTEEN
Ice River Ride

Moss stomped along the top of Farringdon Hill. Salter's shack and the river were behind her. She didn't care how cold it was, it was better than sharing a hut with that cheating thief. How could she have been so stupid? She had known what he was like from the very beginning. From the moment she'd felt him going through her pockets. And yet she'd let herself be taken in by what? His promise to row her to Hampton? Well, that had never happened, had it? He'd used her. She never

211

wanted to see his filthy face again.

The wind ripped at her ears, whirling fistfuls of snow round her as she ploughed towards the light of a building on the other side of the hill. It was an inn. Exhausted, she slumped against its walls.

How could he?

She closed her eyes. She saw Salter, breaking his fish for the hollow-cheeked children, risking his life to save a drowning man, placing a pair of boots next to a crate on the shore. And she saw the hurt in his face. Her words had stung him, sharper than any slap.

But he was a thief and a cheat. And she was alone again. Well, maybe it was meant to be. Now, more than ever, she needed to get to that mill. It was the only place outside the Tower with which she had any connection. The place where she was born and her mother had died. The thought of it filled her with dread and longing, but also with the feeling that if she could only find it, she'd find a part of herself there too.

A candle glow spilt from the open windows of the inn. Each pane framed a picture of firelit people inside. It occurred to her now that Salter's shilling would have bought her a bed and food with enough left over for a cart-ride up the river road.

Moss shook herself. No point in worrying about that now. She had to find somewhere to sleep. Somewhere she wouldn't freeze to death. Then in the morning she'd set off for Hampton. Ask someone the way. Beg for a ride on a cart. Or if she had to, she'd just walk.

She huddled in the doorway and listened to the chatter leaking through the cracks, trying to absorb some warmth from the cosy voices within.

'Old Harry's back in the game then?'

'Ha ha! A Seymour, ain't she?'

'That's what I heard. Bout time someone put those upstart Boleyns in their place. They got where they is too quick and too devious.'

'Can't blame the King for havin a wanderin eye.'

'Can't blame him for wantin a son neither.'

213

'Anne Boleyn had her chance to squeeze out the pups and all she could manage was a girl.'

'My old mare out to pasture could have done better!'

It seemed the people of the city were no different to the people of the Tower. If there was a chance to tittle-tattle about the Queen, they did, slobbering over their gossip like dogs on a well-chewed bone.

The snow was still blowing wild. Though Moss was reluctant to leave the shelter of the doorway, she set off once more. A silver moon soaked the top of the hill in bitter blue light. It made no sense to stay up here where the wind blew coldest. Moss squinted into the moonlight. There were several tracks leading down the hill. So she picked one and followed it. It was a mule track; a steep channel ploughed into the hill by centuries of livestock trudging to market. The track was a gutter of compacted ice with high walls of rock-solid frozen earth. It was so slippery that Moss spent more time on her backside than on her feet.

By the time she reached the foot of the hill, she

wondered if she was covered in bruises, but her body was wet with snow and so numb that she couldn't feel the knocks at all. The memory of that night in the fish crate nipped at her heels. It felt ten times colder tonight. Moss knew that if she went to sleep in the open, it might be a sleep from which she did not wake.

On the frozen river, the spit-fires had burned out and the stalls were packing up. The few people left on the ice pulled their cloaks tight and made for the banks. Moss stepped on to the river and began to walk. The wind bit into her face. She wrapped her arms round her body, curling her freezing fingers into fists and pressing them against any patch of warmth she could feel through her dress. Above her, the sky opened up, vast indigo blue, and the stars were cold, hard stones that gave her no comfort at all.

Keep walking, Moss told herself. If she could walk all night, then maybe she could last until the morning.

It began to snow. Soft flakes that clung to her dress. Prickles of frost jabbing her ribs. On she walked. The wool of her dress soaked up the wet and became a blanket of ice. She walked on still, her feet unfeeling, leaden in the crunching snow. The wind was picking up now, driving into her face until her eyes stung, pushing at her body as if to force it down into the snow beneath her feet. Her eyes were heavy. Strange, thought Moss, that she would feel like lying down and going to sleep. A few moments' rest couldn't hurt? She wouldn't sleep. Just close her eyes. Curl up. A little rest, that's all she needed. She stumbled on. There was nothing now, just snow. The ground came up to meet her. Had she fallen? Her hands clawed in front of her. She felt her knees scrape ice and realised she was crawling. Just a few more paces, then sleep surely? Her feeble fingers clutched something hard and low.

'Ow!'

Her head butted a large and solid object. Holding on to whatever it was, Moss pulled herself up and patted the bulk in front of her. Was it wood? A boat? She felt the lip of a curved open side. Leaning heavily against it, she half fell into it and felt softness embrace her numb body. She didn't know where she was and she didn't care. All that mattered now was sleep.

'Too cold? TOO COLD?!'

Angry words poked Moss awake.

'I'll give you *too cold!*'

She opened her eyes and blinked. All around her was dark. And warm.

'What were you thinking!'

She was just about to sit up when she realised the words were not for her.

'Idiot boy!'

'It was a blizzard, Mr Kimber. I swear, I thought it would freeze me to a stump –'

'Oh, you did, did you? Well, when *I've* finished tanning your hide, you'll wish it had!'

Moss lay very still. She was curled on her side in a tight, cramped space. The memory of last night was as faint as mist. The blizzard. So cold. Crawling in the snow. Sleep. And now here. Where was she? Beneath her and on either side she felt hard wood. She reached up. Above her was something soft and thick. Like fur. She wriggled on to all fours and pushed her head against the soft roof. A chink of daylight was poking through one end. Carefully, she parted the chink with her fingers and peeped out.

A short-cloaked man in leather breeches stood on the ice. In front of him, with his back to Moss, was a boy. Behind them both were three sleighs.

Moss ran her fingers over the wooden floor, feeling it rise to a smooth seat beside her. Was this a *sleigh*? Somehow, she had managed to crawl up here last night in the darkness and the blinding snow and had fallen asleep in the well of the seat.

Outside, the sleighmaster was still bellowing. 'And if I ever catch you leaving the sleighs unguarded again, I'll give you a whipping that'll rip the hide from your breeches! Now get back to the stables and make yourself useful. That idiot Tom Wells is more fool than you. He fed the horses mouldy oats last night and now the slop runs from their backsides like a yellow river.'

The boy hurried off and the sleighmaster began brushing the snow from the sleighs. He still had his back to her. She had to get out of this thing before he found her.

Gently she lifted the fur and slid slowly out of the sleigh on to the ice. Crouching behind it, she looked around. Everything was unfamiliar. It was the riverbank, but not the one she knew. Rising from the river in front of her was a wall of twinkling windows. A gentle ramp ran down one side of the wall to where the sleighs were tethered, one silver, two brown and the one she was hiding in.

A robed man appeared on the ramp and crunched his way through the snow to the bottom. Moss dived under the sleigh.

'Bring down the horses, Kimber! The King and

Queen will be travelling shortly. Separate sleighs.'

'Yes, sir,' said the sleighmaster. 'But I thought –'

'It doesn't matter what you thought. They will ride separately. The King in the silver. Queen Anne may have . . .' He cast his eye over the sleighs and pointed directly at Moss. 'That one there. The black.'

'Yes, sir.'

'Be brisk now, Kimber. They leave for Hampton at one o'clock.'

Hampton? Moss couldn't believe her ears. She slipped further under the sleigh and heard the sleighmaster follow the other man back up the ramp.

Hampton!

She wriggled on to her back. There was actually quite a lot of room beneath the sleigh. The underbelly curved upwards, a smooth, high arch supporting the seat above. Two ornately carved boards hung down the sides, like curtains. The weight of the sleigh rested on two smooth runners, braced across the width by three slim lengths of wood. Moss leant on one. The brace creaked but took her weight.

A little thought crawled out from somewhere inside her head. This sleigh was going to Hampton. Could she somehow go with it?

Easing herself on to the wooden braces, she lay across them on her back and dug her feet against the front of the sleigh. She gripped the supports that joined the runners to the seat. It wasn't exactly comfortable, but who cared? Wherever this sleigh was going, there had to be a chance the Hampton Wheel might be somewhere nearby. And it would be a lot quicker than walking.

Before long, Kimber returned with four greys, followed by stable boys leading a procession of other horses. He barked out orders and after a great deal of confusion it seemed the horses had been harnessed. Moss felt her sleigh move as someone climbed aboard. Wedged on her back, she could see many feet now, robes sweeping down the ramp.

'Make way for His Majesty, King Henry,' boomed a voice. The swirling robes parted and a pair of stout, purple-hosed legs strode across the ice.

Strides that took some effort, observed Moss, and were hampered by a limp. They stopped at the silver sleigh and the robes closed in around them.

'Get off me, you fussers!' growled a voice. 'I'm no invalid! I'll take any one of you in the tiltyard, blindfold, with one arm tied behind my back! Now leave me be!'

The robes stepped back and Moss heard grunts as the stout legs heaved themselves up and into the sleigh.

'Where is she then?'

'She's coming, Your Majesty.' A woman's voice.

'Keep her King waiting, would she? Luther's teeth! I spent less time waiting for a divorce! Damn it, she can catch up. We ride to Hampton *now*.'

Moss heard the snap of a whip and the silver sleigh jerked away. Down the ramp came a flurry of skirts.

'I'm sorry, Your Highness, the King has only just this minute left . . .'

'And I'm to travel alone, in this mournful sleigh?'

came a new voice. 'No matter. Are these horses fast?'

'Yes, Your Highness. Two young Neapolitan coursers that don't mind the ice and will take you swiftly.'

'Good. Then we'll go now.'

Moss felt the sleigh creak above her as the Queen climbed aboard, followed by another lady.

The whip cracked and the horses jerked the sleigh off its spot, nearly tipping Moss on to the ice. She clamped her hands to the supports, stiffening her back, digging her boots hard against the board at the front of the sleigh.

At first it was just a case of holding on and keeping her body central, trying not to lurch too far to one side or the other where she might tumble through the runners on to the ice. The horses trotted slowly, unused to the frozen river with its dusting of snow. The sleigh juddered and lurched, rattling Moss's body up and down on the braces, but she held on tight, stifling her cries over the bumps.

Now the horses were finding their rhythm and

the sleigh began to move faster. The trot became a canter, hooves sending bursts of powdery snow over Moss where she lay. She shook the flakes from her tangle-hair and hung on.

The horses were galloping now, their hooves pounding the uneven ice. The sleigh pitched and tossed, throwing Moss up and down on the braces, knocking the breath from her body. Faster went the sleigh. Above her, the whip snapped and the cry of the sleighman was lost to the rush of air and the hammering hooves. The runners were ripping up the ice, loud as a roaring river, sending a constant spray of ice showering over her, freezing her hands and biting into her face.

Moss held on, numb hands clamped to the wooden supports. The sleigh bucked and jerked, beating her bones until she thought her body would break into a hundred pieces. She tried to keep her grip, but she was losing it. Cold and wet, her fingers were slowly freezing, her grasp cracking. She was slipping sideways. Unable to balance her body, Moss felt herself sliding from the sleigh. The ice rushed towards her, a white blur, carved by the runners that would just as easily slice the fallen limbs of a stowaway girl.

There was a sudden lurch and the sleigh left the ice. For a moment it stopped, snatched by thin air, then walloped back down with a blow to Moss's back that flipped her over on to her side. There she lay, gasping but still onboard.

'Easy now!' The sleighman hauled on the reins and the horses slowed.

As Moss's breath returned, she realised the ride was getting smoother. She curled her hands into her chest, willing them to take any ounce of warmth from her body. The bumps and jolts became fewer. She turned her head and saw fields, dotted with the odd cottage or house. They were out in open countryside now where the snow was untravelled. A bleak, white-covered landscape, where trees outnumbered people. London must be far behind. Above, the Queen and her lady were quiet. How far was it to Hampton? How long had they been travelling? One hour? Two? She had no idea.

Moss wriggled on to her stomach. The ride was quite steady now and if she hadn't been so cold she could almost have drifted off to sleep, lulled by the slice of the runners and the crisp trot of the horses. Her head was heavy. The ice rushed by and she stared at the tracks carved by the runners in the frozen river.

As she gazed down, her eyes were drawn to a darkness in the ice. At first she thought it must be the reflection of the sleigh, but when she looked more carefully she could see that wasn't it.

There was something there. Under the ice. A green-black shadow.

Following the sleigh.

Moss felt a twist in her gut. The shadow was fanning out, extending green-black tendrils that seemed to grasp at the sleigh. She tried to roll on to her back, but her body wouldn't move. Her eyes locked on the coiling, spreading shape. A hand reached out to touch the ice and it took Moss several moments to realise it was her own.

Now the shadow darkened, still racing with the sleigh, but shrinking, as though coming into focus. Moss couldn't tear her gaze from it.

Then she pulled back with a cry. For a single instant there was a face. A woman's face. Broken and jagged under the ice. And then it was gone.

Moss felt the sleigh judder and above her she heard the sleighman call, 'Whoa!' The horses slowed to a walk.

'Something spooked them,' muttered the sleighman. 'Easy now! Nearly there, Your Highness.'

The shadow under the ice was fading. Moss felt her gut untwist, leaving a trembling thought that she pushed away quickly.

'People drown all the time,' she whispered. 'It was a poor drowned one, trapped under the ice.'

Her words, spoken aloud, were almost enough to convince herself.

Almost.

CHAPTER EIGHTEEN
Dragon's Heart

The sleigh came to a gentle stop.

Moss peeked out from underneath. A frost-clad jetty sat square to the bank. Staking a wide path from the jetty were two lines of torches, and though it was still daylight, the torches had been lit. At the end of the path was a golden-turreted gatehouse, five storeys high, draped with flags that slapped the walls in the winter wind. Beyond that, spreading like an elegant brick cake, was an enormous building.

'Here we are, Your Highness,' said the sleighman. 'Hampton Court Palace.'

Palace? Moss remembered Salter's laughter when she'd told him she was trying to get to Hampton. No wonder, if he thought she was heading for a palace.

The Queen disembarked, brushing off the hands of servants. Moss craned forward as far as she dared, trying to get a look at her face, but all she saw was a fur-trimmed cloak, drawn tight, sweeping across the ice to the torchlit path.

Moss felt the sleigh move again. By now her fingers were so numb they would not close. Her body was cold and weak, and it was all she could do to keep her balance while the sleigh slid further down the river. Mercifully, it went slowly and soon it stopped. Peeking out once more, she saw the sleighman knotting a rope to several other sleighs tied together on the ice. Blowing on his hands, he unharnessed the horses and led them towards a set of low buildings that Moss guessed were the stables.

It took some effort to crawl from under the sleigh

and hobble to the bank. There was a lightness to her head and Moss's legs could barely carry her weight. She scoured the bank for any sign of a ruined mill, but all she could see were willows. A sour pain was spreading across her belly and Moss realised she was famished. She couldn't remember when she had last eaten – it felt so long ago. The mill would have to wait. She needed food and right now her best chance of *that* lay in the enormous building at the other end of those flaming torches.

More sleighs were arriving on the river, servants buzzing between the guests and the torchlit path. Away from the path, the bushes offered good cover and Moss reckoned she could get pretty close to the palace without being seen.

Slowly, she crawled through the snow, hoping her movements wouldn't draw the eye of anyone who happened to be looking her way. As she crawled, the pain in her belly grew.

A brick wall bounded the palace. For Moss, who had daily scrambled up and down the Tower battlements, climbing the wall was easy, despite her hunger. She dropped down to the other side quickly. There wasn't a guard in sight.

The clean smell of snow was broken by something wafting through the air – something delicious. Moss followed her nose, letting the sweet, drifting scent lead her to one side of the palace, where steam poured from a cluster of open windows. As she crawled closer, she could hear shouts and cries and the clatter of pans. The sounds of a busy kitchen – and that meant food.

'Keep that stag turning!' shouted someone inside.

'Gawd! Someone open another window! It's hotter than a devil's backside in here!'

The smell of roasting meat filled Moss's nostrils and deep in her gut the hunger gnawed, like a ravenous creature that was eating her from the inside out.

Her head began to fill with pictures of food. The meals she shared with Pa. Bread. Soup. Cheese. Meat. An apple if she was lucky. Simple food, but always three meals a day. Then she thought of the things she'd eaten with Salter. The mutton-raisin pie, crispy sprats fresh from the smoker. The creature bit deeper.

She stopped underneath a small window. With the sweet smell of hot pastry all around her, Moss had only one thing on her mind. For a moment she forgot this was the palace of a king. That the feast being prepared on the other side of those walls was his. That a thieving urchin would be kicked all the way back to the river if she were caught. All that mattered was food. Something to stop that gnawing pain.

Moss reached up to the window, her thin arms pulling her body on to the ledge. The window was small, but so was she. Quietly, she slipped inside, grazing her knees on the stone. It was a long drop to the other side. Easing herself off the ledge, she rolled on to her stomach and, hanging by her fingertips, slid to the ground.

She was in a candlelit room, filled with the rich smell of roasted meat. As her eyes got used to the flickering light, she saw the room was lined with shelves and crammed with tables. On every surface was a platter. Piled on those platters was every kind of bird she could have imagined, still with their heads on, cooked and basted and glistening with butter. It was a strange sight. Stranger still was that each had been plucked, then redressed in a woven cape of its own feathers.

There were green-winged ducks, black chickens, mottled pheasants, plump, speckled partridges, sleek grey geese; and next to the geese was a nest of real bulrushes holding a clutch of downy yellow goslings. There was a peacock cloaked from the throat in tiny feathers of startling blue. There was a dovecote with startled doves peeping from the windows. And in the centre of the room, on a table of its own, sat an enormous gilt platter, as smooth and glassy as a lake. Resting on this golden lake was a pure-white bird, its neck somehow lifted in a long and gentle curve all the way to the black feathers round its beak, a flash of brilliant orange. On the bird's head was a gilded pastry crown, set with sparkling sugar-dipped berries. Beneath the crown, two glassy eyes stared blindly at Moss.

Moss blinked. Her stomach growled up at her, but she backed away from the unseeing bird with its creepy eyes and bumped into a table laden with cooked pigeons.

Bread first then morals.

They were Salter's words, but it was her own voice she heard, ringing inside her head. Before she could think, her hand shot to the table; she snatched a pigeon and jammed as much of it into her mouth as she could. She gulped down the succulent flesh, then choked half of it back up. The warm juices ran through her fingers on to her dress. It tasted so good she wanted to laugh. As she gobbled and gulped, the pain in her stomach melted away. Suddenly she understood what Salter had meant. Against hunger, nothing else seemed to matter.

Here she was. A thief. Just like him.

'The goslings go up first, Stubbs . . .'

Voices and footsteps were approaching. Somewhere outside. In the corridor.

Moss glanced up at the small window. It was too high for her to reach and there was no time to push a table against it.

The voices were coming closer. Towards the room. A man, talking hurriedly.

'Goslings first, then the boar's head from the meat larder. Fetch your kitchen boys. I want four of them ready with the peacock.'

There were two doors in the bird room. Moss picked one and edged towards it. She should have been out of there and running, looking for a place to hide, but for a split second she hesitated. On the table next to the pigeons, someone had left an apron and cap. Quick as a cat, she grabbed them. Darting through the doorway, she sprang back against the wall.

She was in a snow-covered alley.

From the larder came a wail.

'STUBBS!' Followed by the clatter of feet.

235

Moss didn't wait to hear more. Fumbling with the apron, she tied it round her waist, tugging the cap over her tangle-hair. She walked briskly down the alley, thinking she'd draw less attention to herself if she looked like she knew where she was going. Through another doorway was a covered corridor, criss-crossed with scores of servants rushing in and out of the many rooms on either side. She ducked under two men carrying a large platter of fish and found herself in a kitchen bursting with people, every one of them screaming or scowling as they chopped, stirred, poked, fetched and carried. Everywhere was food. Vegetables thrown into pots, meat slapped on to slabs, pies steaming on tables and a roasting stag in a fireplace the size of a small house. There was more food here than Moss had seen in her entire life. It was a feast for a giant, she thought. And judging by the harassed looks on everyone's faces, this giant did not take kindly to a late dinner.

Moss weaved in and out of the bustle, emerging

in a dark, wide corridor behind a group of kitchen boys. On their shoulders the boys carried a huge wooden platter. On it was a whole hog, dripping with honey. A cook was shooing them to the foot of a staircase. Several girls scurried behind with jugs of sauce and plates of bread.

'Get that lot up to the Great Hall now! No shilly-shallying!'

Moss bent her head and tried to melt into the gaggle of servants. Too distracted to notice a girl going somewhere she shouldn't, no one gave her a second glance. She fell in step and when one of them dropped her spoons, Moss picked them up. The grateful girl looked back and nodded thanks as the hog-bearers set off up a staircase.

At the top, the line stopped. A liveried footman stood by an arched door.

'Put what you're carrying on the long table, then straight back out and down the way you came. No gawping. Understand?'

They all nodded.

Moss stepped through the door and almost toppled backwards.

The room was the size of a cathedral, as high as the sky itself. Swirling on the polished floor were dancing courtiers, dwarfed by the soaring beams that arched like ribs against the ceiling. And in the midst of it all, on a raised platform not ten feet away, was the giant himself. Henry, the King of England. And his Queen, Anne Boleyn.

Shoehorned into a high throne, the King lounged back, his legs splayed, puffed with robes that made him as wide as he was tall. A plumed hat nested on his head, which he held stiffly, blunt as a box. He moved restlessly, his body turned away from the Queen. Next to him, she was half his size, a slight figure in a purple velvet dress, her dark hair scraped back under a French hood. There was a pained look to her face. Moss could see the King's eyes flicking lazily across the platform to a woman who stood between two young men. The men wore pleated capes and their buckles were polished. But the woman's dress was plain and her face was as pale as dough. A loaf of bread between two sugared cakes, thought Moss. Her ears caught the whispers of the courtiers.

Jane Seymour . . . see how the King looks at her. . . See how she stands, so modest between her brothers . . . The Seymours! The Seymours are on the up.

Moss felt a nudge in the ribs from the kitchen girl, so she dropped her eyes to the floor, following the line of servants to the long table on one side of the hall. As she laid her spoons next to a jug there was a blast of trumpets.

Everything stopped. The courtiers hushed. The Great Hall was quiet.

A robed man stepped to the side of the platform and raised his arms. 'My lords, ladies and gentlemen of the court! In honour of this day, the Feast Day of St Valentine, a masque!'

Behind the King, a stone-eyed man smiled grimly. Moss swallowed a little cry as she recognised the Duke of Norfolk. The one whose cold words about the Queen's baby had made her shiver.

239

The trumpets blasted again. At the far end, a high curtain parted.

There was a roar, like a thousand pairs of bellows. A plume of yellow fire shot into the hall and the courtiers screamed. The fire blasted again, filling the air with grey smoke. When the smoke cleared, there was an astonished gasp from all in the room. Moss gaped, her throat dry at the impossible sight before her now.

It was a dragon.

Shimmering, silver-scaled and red-winged, it was the size of five horses. Its monstrous jaws opened wide and gnashed. The dragon lumbered forward, rattling its scales, webbed wings unfurling. It roared again. More screams came from the courtiers and in reply the dragon spat out another blast of flames.

Moss found herself gripping the arm of the kitchen girl, who grinned and whispered, 'It ain't real, don't fret yerself. Look.' She pointed at the dragon's feet. Beneath its coat of glittering scales turned six wheels. Between the wheels, Moss could see booted feet slipping and sliding on the polished floor. She heard the creaking of wood and the grunts of men as they strained to propel the beast forward. Its head was bright with silver scales, polished, like one of Pa's new steel swords. And now she looked closely, its clanging jaws seemed familiar. Jagged with dagger-sharp metal teeth.

'Oh!' A memory clicked. Those were the jaws Pa had been hammering that day in the forge. Had he made this dragon's head? Was this his big secret project? She couldn't help smiling. A dragon's head made by Pa! Here in the palace of the King! Her stomach did a little somersault and she looked around, half expecting to see Pa in the audience. And when she couldn't see him, she felt a stab of disappointment. She wondered where he was now. In the forge? Out looking for her? She flushed with guilt and tried not to think about the fact she'd been gone for so many days and Pa was most likely out of his mind with worry.

In the Great Hall, the courtiers were edging

forward and their hush grew into an excited babble.

Red-winged . . . A Tudor dragon . . .

The trumpets screeched above Moss's head and there was a loud bang as the wide doors at the end of the hall flew open. Courtiers scattered in all directions. To the astonishment of all, a real horse galloped down the length of the Great Hall. On its back was a knight, dazzling head to toe in gold and silver armour, heavy as a wine barrel, judging by the snorts from the horse. The knight held a long lance high, its tip brushing the flags that dangled from the beams. As he turned his horse at the end of the hall, he lowered the lance and the dragon roared.

The courtiers cheered. The knight clanked his armoured heels against the horse's flanks and with a cry he galloped towards the dragon.

'Oooh!' gasped the courtiers as the lance struck the dragon's wing. The force of his thrust ripped a hole in the webbing, splitting the wing from the dragon's back and dragging it half the length of the hall.

The dragon spat fire and, as the knight turned

his horse again, Moss thought it must be terrifying for whoever was inside that beast. She could hear them pumping bellows like crazy and wondered that they didn't set the costume alight. She hoped at least they'd be able to singe the knight's cloak.

There was a cheer. The knight charged down the hall again, full tilt, lance poised. The dragon roared, and this time when the knight struck he drove the lance through the gaping metal jaws of the beast, shattering through the back of its head in an explosion of steel scales.

The dragon groaned. There was a cracking of wood and it sank to its knees. Its mouth sparked. Its head trembled. Moss knew the dragon wasn't real, yet there was something pitiful in the ruin of this groaning beast.

Now the knight clambered down from his horse, armour clanking. He drew his sword and strode over to the dragon. Carving a wide arc in the air, he brought the sword down hard, slashing a deep gash in its side. A river of red silk ran from the wound and the room gasped, as though it were the dragon taking its last breath.

The knight knelt and reached inside the creature. When his hand emerged, it held something red and soft. A heart-shaped cushion.

'Ahhh,' breathed the crowd.

The room was quiet, save for the clanking knight as he approached the King's platform, holding the cushion high above his head. He knelt before the King.

'Your Majesty.'

The King motioned for the knight to climb the platform.

'A fight well fought, good knight.' The King's voice boomed across the Great Hall. 'Tell me, what do you bring for your King?'

'The heart of the dragon, Your Majesty.' The knight bowed low.

The King signalled to the knight. A flick of his finger. The knight rose with the cushion and walked to where the plain woman stood between her two brothers. He knelt, stretched out his hands and offered her the heart cushion. She took it and her dough-cheeks flushed pink.

Then the King threw his head back and guffawed. He hooted until his ginger beard was wet with spit. As if this was suddenly the funniest joke in the world, the court erupted with laughter too.

But Moss wasn't watching the King or the courtiers. She was looking at Queen Anne Boleyn, whose pinched face had paled as the other lady had taken the cushion. That heart meant something. Whatever it was, it gave the Queen painful thought.

The stone-eyed uncle smiled a grim smile. The King wiped the spit from his beard. And again Moss shivered and thought she would not trade places with the Queen for all the riches in the world.

The Queen got up, made a curtsey to the King and walked down the platform steps. As she went, the King clapped his hands and the Great Hall filled with a stout melody. Moss saw the Queen close her eyes, as if trying to shut out the music and the whispers, before disappearing through a wide door.

The Queen's exit shook Moss from this dreamlike spectacle. As the room came back into focus, she was suddenly aware the other servants had gone and she was now standing alone at the long table. The liveried footman at the arched door was glaring at her, motioning furiously for her to return to the kitchen. She saw him speak quickly to two other footmen. She backed away and the sight of them striding silently towards her made her dart underneath the long table, scrabbling out the other side. There were a few surprised cries as she slipped in and out of the crowding courtiers, but she was eel-quick. Before the footmen could reach her, she'd dashed through the door at the end of the hall.

Down a wide wooden staircase Moss scuttled, vaulting three steps at a time, courtiers flashing past. What *was* she doing here? She cursed herself for stowing away on the sleigh, cursed her hunger and her boldness. She sprinted across a cloistered courtyard, through a doorway, and found herself back in the larder of birds.

She pulled off the apron and cap and was about to scramble through the other door, when something stopped her. Still on its gilt lake was the long-necked bird, draped in the cloak of white feathers. This was how a King lived. In a palace of stuffed birds, silver dragons, charging horses and roasting stags. So much wealth. So much food. With the birds in this room alone, you could feed a whole riverbank of children *and* give them each a feather cloak to keep out the cold.

She reached up to the neck of the white bird and tugged. The cloak of feathers fell to the floor. Moss snatched it up, bundling it into a ball. She darted through the doorway and scrambled through a cloistered walkway, spilling out into an expanse of snow.

She didn't stop running until she'd reached the outer wall. Only then did she look back. No one had followed her.

CHAPTER NINETEEN
The Queen and the Little Swan

Moss stuck close to the wall, shivering. It was too high to climb, so she followed it away from the palace, her head aching with cold. She longed for a familiar face. Nell, Salter – even Two-Bellies would have been a comfort. But most of all, she wished she was with Pa.

Pa. She could almost feel his big bear-arms, wrapping her in a blanket. Leading her to the fire. Setting a bowl of soup in her hands. She thought of him as she'd last seen him a few days ago, scouring the riverbank, looking for her, calling her name. Then she remembered him stumbling, on his knees on the cold shingle. Why hadn't she run to him? Helped him? Because he'd lied to her? Because he'd made a life for them both in a terrible place, doing terrible things?

Everything I've done, I did for you.

Pa's words, his words to her on the day she left, came whispering, filling her head. She tried to push them away, but they would not go.

Everything I've done . . .

All was quiet and pink-white – a thick coverlet of snow, lit by the setting sun.

The bird-feather cloak was soft in her hands and Moss realised she would be warmer if she put it on. She shook it out, unfurling the feathers and smoothing them flat. They were the colour of snow. Moss clasped the cloak round her neck. It was a little tight, but warmer than two blankets, and though it trailed on the ground it stayed dry.

She moved slowly along the base of the wall. In the distance, she could make out the drooping tops of willow trees. That way was the river. Perhaps there was still enough light to try and find the mill? Sticking to the brickwork, Moss followed the meandering line of the wall towards the river. For anyone who looked, it would have been an odd sight. The tangle-head of a girl on a cone of feathers, gliding across the snow.

At the wall's end, she met another. To her left was a large garden. To her right, set into the red bricks, was a door. Moss pushed it open, the creak of old wood breaking the silence. On the other side was a sight so strange that at first Moss thought she must be dreaming.

Rising from the ground in neat rows was an army of wooden poles. On each crouched a creature on its hind legs, carved from wood and painted in stark, bright colours. There was a red dragon, gripping its pole with powerful claws. Next to it was a wild-eyed greyhound, then a crowned lion. There was a white-winged falcon with a golden beak. And further down the line was a strange, twisted creature with the body of a goat and the tail of a lion.

Moss crept slowly towards the nearest – a brutish black bull that stared down at her with bulging eyes. She backed away.

There was a rustle behind her. An echo of footsteps. Moss whipped round.

No one.

Then she heard a voice. Clear and cutting through the dusk.

'A stranger who dares to walk this garden.'

Moss wheeled round again.

'A thing cloaked in feathers. Are you girl or swan?'

Walking towards her was a woman, her jewelled purple dress brushing the snow, a sight almost as unreal as the crouching creatures.

Moss's heart almost jumped from her chest. It was the Queen. She backed away, although there wasn't really anywhere to go.

'Stop!' said the Queen. 'Don't . . . leave.' Her eyes

were bright berry-brown and pierced Moss with a curious gaze. 'There's no one here. No guards. And I daresay you are no more threat to me than I am to you. Tell me, do you know who I am?'

Moss nodded.

'Then you have the advantage, feathered girl.'

The Queen walked round Moss, circling her like a cat.

'Who are you, little swan? A restless ghost from my dreams? A jester sent to taunt me?'

The Queen gave a brittle laugh. It shook her slender head and shoulders. 'Perhaps you are an escapee from my uncle's masque? A little-necked bird for the knight to slay bravely with his sword?'

Moss didn't know what to say. She was wearing a stolen cloak. She'd eaten from the King's larder. She was a thief. This could only end badly. She backed round the dragon pole.

'Don't worry,' said the Queen, 'I won't send you back up there to that gaudy spectacle. And if your absence makes my uncle cross, I hope he pops an eye!' As she spoke these words, the Queen's face lit up and in it Moss saw mischief and fun and none of the pain that was there before. 'Can you speak? Do you have a name?'

'My Lady . . . Your Majesty . . . Highness . . .. my name is Moss.' Moss bobbed a squat curtsey and the Queen frowned slightly at the strangeness of her manner.

'You have not spent much time at court then?'

Moss shook her head. 'None . . . really.'

'But you were there today, at the masque?'

Moss nodded.

'So tell me, what did you think of His Majesty?'

Moss was at a loss to know what to say. 'He was . . . like a giant.'

'Ha!' The Queen seemed to find this funny. 'Yes, a giant! The appetite of a giant he certainly has. A giant's merciless hand too. But I am not afraid of him.' She frowned. 'Though he could at least have waited until I'd left the room. The heart of the Tudor dragon! I suppose you saw that ridiculous gesture?'

'The red cushion?' said Moss. 'What did that mean?'

'What indeed? The Tudor dragon is Henry himself. Slain by the knight. The knight is Love. His heart given to another. Did you see her? Standing between those two grasping brothers of hers. They're almost as bad as my own family!' The Queen gave a bitter chuckle. 'Pale Jane Seymour. She's not so different from me, you know. Traded like a roll of silk from a merchant's ship. Tell me, do you have a family?'

'Yes,' said Moss, 'I have Pa – I mean my father.'

'And does your father love you?'

The question caught Moss unawares. Did Pa *love* her? He'd lied to her. He'd taken away her freedom.

'I don't know,' said Moss. '*How* would I know?'

'Trust me, you know,' said the Queen. 'You know when they care. My family, for example, wouldn't know love if it jumped up and bit them on the nose. The fortune of our family is everything. Money, land, titles, power. People . . . people are nothing.

Your worth will be measured by your husband's wealth and position. So marry up. That's what Uncle Norfolk says. Is your father like that?'

'Not exactly.'

'You are lucky. My father and my uncle, they'd marry their daughters to a gang of knife-wielding murderers if it put the Norfolks in the King's favour.'

Moss thought back to the first glimpse she'd caught of the King and Queen on the sleigh that evening of the Frost Fair. The Queen's troubled face. How she'd left the Great Hall and no one with her.

'But you are Queen. You have done what your family wanted. Don't they care for you at all?'

'Ha! They care when there is some advantage for *them*. But now . . .' The Queen looked up at the sunset sky, turning from pink to deep red. 'Now the ship is sinking and every one of them swims for shore. Like the rats they are.'

'Oh,' said Moss. 'What about the King? Doesn't he love you?'

The Queen's eyebrows shot up in surprise.

'A bold question, little swan.' But she seemed amused by it nevertheless. 'All my life I've fought to be myself. I read Greek and Latin. I learnt to hunt with my brother. I can shoot a bow and play cards as well as any man. It was never my way to sit with the gossips, needling at a tapestry. I've never wanted a quiet life. When my daughter was born, I defied those meddling courtiers and fed her myself. Unheard of for a queen! I say what I think and I make people laugh with my wit. And for a while I made the King laugh. He likes to laugh, you know. He likes fun and mischief, just as I do. He had never met anyone quite like me, I can tell you.'

Listening to Queen Anne Boleyn, to her spirited, defiant words, Moss could well believe it.

'So *yes* is the answer to your question. The King loved me once. A giant's love. Strong and passionate. I gave him good company. I gave him a daughter, my beautiful Elizabeth, my little princess redhead whom I love more than my own life. But now it seems the one thing he really wants, I cannot give him. A son and heir.'

'So . . . so . . .'

'So perhaps my great adventure is over. It will end soon for me, one way or another.'

The Queen walked over to the white carved falcon and flicked it on the beak.

'The emblem of the Plantagenets.' She gestured to the rest of the carved creatures. 'The bull of Clarence, the Beaufort yale, the greyhound of Richmond. These are the old families of England. Ha! I shook them up, I can tell you! They sneered at me when I came to court. They like a lady meek, not bold. I gave them cheek and they hated me for not being like them. Now they regroup and they wait.'

'What do they wait for?'

'For this Queen to fall and another to take her place.'

The Queen looked at Moss and Moss met her straight gaze.

'I do not know how this will end. But I'll tell

you something.' The Queen raised her chin. 'I don't regret a thing. Can you guess why?'

Moss was quiet for a moment. 'I think I can,' she said.

The Queen looked surprised and Moss took a deep breath.

'I think . . . I think, what is the point of life if you cannot somehow be yourself.'

'Go on,' said the Queen.

'You said you didn't want a quiet life, but a great adventure. And that is what you found. In spite of your family and all that they wanted from you. Somehow we find a way . . . to be ourselves. To make our own way. Without that we suffocate. We might as well be dead.'

The beasts stared down at Moss, their silent snarls and screeches trapped in their carved mouths.

'Nicely put, little swan.' The Queen was behind her. Moss could feel the bright berry eyes drill the back of her head. 'Spoken like someone who is looking for adventure herself. Trying to make her own way in this world.'

Moss nodded.

Queen Anne opened a velvet pouch that hung by her side and took something out. She extended her hand to Moss. In it was a small silver bird.

'A pretty charm that I would have passed to my daughter Elizabeth. But it's brought me little luck,' said the Queen. 'Take it. It is silver and of fine craftsmanship. If nothing else, you can sell it.'

She placed it in the palm of Moss's hand.

The bird glinted in the half-light. Its talons were clasped together, its beak open, as though calling out.

'Be careful, the beak is sharp and will cut your finger if you forget it is so.'

Carefully, Moss tucked the silver bird into her pocket.

'Spread your wings, little swan,' said the Queen. 'But while you fly, think on this. Hold on to love.

Wherever you can find it. Do not let it go. It is a most precious thing.'

'I . . . Thank you,' said Moss.

'Now then, did you know this is the King's own garden?'

'The King's garden?'

'No one should enter this garden except the King himself. So you see, you and I are both somewhere we really shouldn't be.' Again the mischievous smile flitted across the Queen's lips. 'I am glad to have shared this time with you. Now we will go our own ways. Tell me, where *were* you going?'

'I was looking for the river.'

The Queen laughed. 'Of course! Why not! A swan belongs on the river. Follow me then.'

She led Moss through a door at the other end of the garden and on to a tall stone gateway, flanked by two soldiers, halberds crossed.

'Let this girl pass,' said the Queen briskly.

The soldiers looked Moss up and down, but parted to let her pass. She stepped through the gate

and looked back to say goodbye. But the Queen had
gone.

The riverbank, away from the palace, was a long,
gentle bend. Moss plunged into the snow, glad to
feel the cold chewing at her face. The past night
and day felt unreal. A waking dream of sleigh rides,
dragons and spirited Queens with ruthless families.
What she'd seen and heard had shocked her. Queen
Anne did not want pity, yet Moss was sorry for her,
deserted by her own grasping family. She knew Pa
would never, ever do anything like that.

She thought of that day she had run away. Of
Pa's broken face as she'd pushed past him. Then,
out of the blue, Salter's words popped into her
head. *Sometimes you don't know what you've got, till you
ain't got it no more.*

'Oh!' Moss came to a sudden stop.

The gentle curve of the river was broken by
a ruined building with an odd-shaped chimney,

slumped on the bank like a tired soldier. Next to it was a great wooden wheel, its splintered paddles trapped in the crusted ice.

A waterwheel.

On a bend of the river. Just as Nell had described. A crooked chimney. A great shattered wheel. Moss stumbled towards it in lolloping strides, kicking up snow as she went.

But when she got to the tumble of grey stone she stopped. The air that had been still and quiet now hummed. A tuneless wind was whistling through the gaps in the stones, a stirring of voices from this long-forgotten ruin.

She picked her way through the fallen rubble. As Moss drew close to the wheel it creaked, as if it too had been woken by her presence. She reached out to touch the crumbling wood. It was damp and slippery. The ancient paddles that had once ploughed the water were still, gripped by the frozen river.

This was the place. This dark corner. The Hampton Wheel. The place where she'd begun and her mother had died. Maybe somewhere in the cold shadows of this mill a little of her voice might linger? Something of her mother that Moss might cling to. Her heart ached for it. Something that she could carry with her. *Hers*, not Pa's.

Moss felt her chest heave. She tried to picture her mother, searched for any trace of her in the ice river. A hand. A look. The sound of her gasps. Anything.

But all she could see was Pa.

Pa's strong arms pulling her clear of the water. Pa cradling her against his chest. Heaving himself and the baby out of the icy river. Casting around desperately for something to keep the tiny child warm.

Beneath the ice, the water was dark.

A breeze stirred the feathers on Moss's cloak. The humming stopped. But there was no whisper of her mother. Nothing at all.

Then Moss sat down and did something she had never done her whole life long. She began to cry. Small tears at first. She tried to choke them back down, but they wouldn't stop. And in the end she gave in and wept. She sat in the snow and wept for her mother. Whose arms she would never feel. Whose voice she would never hear. And for Pa. Who'd promised his wife he'd keep their child safe. And who had done his best to keep that promise.

CHAPTER TWENTY
The Riverwitch

Moss sat alone on the bank. Her face was numb, the salt crust of her tears frozen to her cheeks.

In front of her stretched the river. A long, wide ribbon of ice. If she followed it, it would take her back to London.

Levering herself down the bank with one arm on the waterwheel, Moss stepped on to the ice. There was a *crick-crack*. Then silence.

The sun had set now. The only light was from

a low moon that sent twisted fingers of shadow stretching from the trees on to the frozen water. Moss found herself stepping over them, treading softly. On a night like this and in a place like this, it was easy to believe anyone or anything might be watching.

It was so quiet. Just the gentle crunch of her boots and a slow creak that seemed to feel its way across the ice to where she walked. Deep below her feet a low groan echoed. It was as if the river was humming. She banged her ears, thinking her head must be conjuring noise to fill the silence.

Then something shook her and she felt her knees begin to buckle. A strange dizzy sensation made her stagger backwards.

The ice was moving.

It was maybe twenty paces to the bank. Her boots slipped as she tried to run to safety and she fell to her knees, the ice shifting beneath her. She looked down and saw a dark streak approaching under the frozen water. A lightning streak of green-black that zigzagged towards her.

Beneath her, the frozen river was coming to life. Breaking and splintering and crying out as though in pain, the ice opened up into a great chasm, exposing the black water below. As her legs were pulled in opposite directions, straddling two pieces of broken ice, Moss dived for the larger one and her body smacked down hard, knocking the breath from her lungs. She scrabbled to clear her legs from the freezing water. The ice lurched and Moss found herself sliding, fingers clawing pointlessly on the ice crust. She threw herself forward, rolling the weight of her body away from the edge, trying to rebalance the plate of ice.

Crawling to the middle, she scrambled to her knees, gasping. The ice on which she knelt was still rocking, but the water underneath was calmer now. She shuffled a few feet towards the bank, but stopped again when the ice began to tip. Her breath came quicker now in panicky gulps. How was she going to get to the bank? As she cast around the river wildly, she noticed that where her legs had scraped the snow, the ice underneath was almost transparent. Brushing more snow away with her hand, Moss stared through it into the fathomless river below. Dark shapes swirled beneath her. Tendrils of weed perhaps? She couldn't tell. Mesmerised by the whirling shapes and by an eerie green light that swirled with them, she crouched down and pressed her face close to the ice.

Something stirred beneath the weeds. Moss blinked, then reeled back with a cry. Staring up at her through the ice was a face.

Pale, blank, no smile or frown. A poor drowned woman. The face she'd seen before. A dead face. An undead face. A skull-like face lit by strange candle eyes. Hair coiling all around. Fronds of grey skin hanging from her cheeks like a bridal veil. A mouth, half-torn, teeth rooted in bare bone. Moss could not wrench her gaze away from this pale drowned woman. Or from her lips, which seemed to want to speak. Moss stared and, as she stared, slowly she began to make out the shape and meaning of the words that came silently from the woman's torn lips.

'River daughter . . .'

And Moss knew the words were for her.

'You . . . belong to me.'

CRACK!

A hand shot through the ice and Moss exploded into life, kicking out at the clawed fingers. They seized her cloak and pulled. Moss jerked back, then tore the clasp from her throat. The ice lurched. Moss jumped to her feet, feathers flying. Across the ice she ran as it swayed and tipped, leaping from one chunk to the next, her boots skimming the water, throwing herself head first from the last piece of ice into the deep snow of the bank. She scrabbled on to her back in time to see the hand shrink back into the hole, dragging the cloak of feathers with it.

Laughter echoed from the river.

'Get away from me, whoever, whatever you are!' Moss cried.

269

The laughter came again, teasing her.

Moss knew though. Knew exactly who this undead woman was.

As she lay, cushioned by the snowy bank, she saw the plates of ice come apart. Slowly, waist-high from the ink-black river, rose the tattered form of the Riverwitch.

Around her fanned a dress. Of cloth or weed, Moss couldn't tell. It was as torn as the fronds of skin on her face. The Witch turned slowly and two candle eyes looked down at Moss.

Moss knew she should run. She could be up and over that bank rabbit-quick. But the Riverwitch's flickering eyes held her and she stayed where she was. After all Nell's stories. After all Pa had said. Superstitious nonsense? No, this creature, this Witch of the Rivers, was real. She felt her world slide, a heap of stones at her feet.

The water was quiet now. The ice had settled into a flat sheet. The only thing that moved was the Riverwitch's mouth, opening slowly, as though it caused her great pain.

'The one who came too soon. The one who should have died.' Her words cut like a blade through the stillness. 'The river daughter. Now the *Executioner's* daughter, are you not? Promised to me by your mother. Kept away from me by your father.'

Somewhere inside, Moss found her voice, though it was barely more than a croak.

'Pa only . . . He only did it to keep me safe.'

'Foolish he was, to think he could keep you locked in a tower forever.' Her lips peeled back, baring teeth and bone. 'A child that is born to the river shall return to the river.'

'Why?' said Moss. 'What do you want from me?'

'What every mother wants from her child.'

'I'm not your child.'

The Riverwitch's teeth parted. A hollow smile.

'But why didn't you just take me when you could?' said Moss. 'The day I fell in. I thought it was a drowned woman, but it was . . . *you.*'

The candle eyes flickered. 'A promise should

be kept,' said the Witch. 'I gave your father twelve years. Time enough to grow to love you. As I did my own son. Time enough to feel the pain of losing his only child. As I did mine.'

An icy hand seemed to clutch at Moss's heart. 'Is that why you do this?' she said. 'To cause so much pain?'

'When you have lost the one you love,' said the Riverwitch, 'then pain is all you know.'

Moss thought back to Nell's story. The miller's daughter, whose son had been taken from her, whose grief was too much to bear, who'd thrown herself from the millwheel to die in the cold river.

'Your son,' said Moss. 'It was wrong what they did. Taking him away. But that doesn't make it right to take the children of others.'

The Riverwitch laughed and the creaking ice seemed to laugh with her. 'I fill my rivers with the bodies of children and they comfort me.'

'You take them and drown them, you mean.'

'I call them, but they never come to me. So I

take them, I wrap my arms round them, feel their warm, beating hearts. They struggle. They shouldn't struggle so hard . . .'

She drifted towards the bank and when she was just a few feet from Moss she stopped and held out her bone-thin arms.

'I do not mean for them to drown, but they struggle so. I hold them, I hold them till they are still. And when they struggle no more, they are mine to hold.'

The Witch raised herself up a little further. Flaps of skin dripped riverwater and it ran down her skull-face. Her eyes flickered liquid green, more like tears than flame. Moss could see their reflection, two sorrowful pools in the black river.

Edging slowly back, Moss forced down the horror of what she had learnt. She could almost hear the cries of drowning children, the screams of the miller's daughter and the pounding of horses' hooves, mixed with the wailing of the son for the arms of his mother.

As slowly as she had risen, the Riverwitch sank down and lay back in the river. 'Two days you have. Then you will come to me.'

'And if I don't?'

'*He* will find you.'

The Riverwitch closed her eyes and Moss watched her tattered body sink deep below the surface, until all that was left was the rippling water.

CHAPTER TWENTY-ONE
Snatcher on the Shore

Lost in her thoughts, Moss almost didn't hear the cry from upriver.

'*Hey!*'

Someone was calling.

'*Leatherboots! Is that you?*'

She squinted into the half-light to where the voice was coming from and saw a wiry arm, waving at her from the bank at the bend in the river.

Salter?

Moss sprang up the bank and ran, her heart

thumping and soaring, yelling as she raced to meet him.

'Salter! Salter!' No other word would come, but she didn't care. She had never been so pleased to see anyone in all her life.

It was midnight by the time they reached Salter's shack. They'd walked the bank as far as an inn, Moss quiet, the words of the Riverwitch stalking her thoughts. At the inn Salter had fixed a ride in a cart bound for London. Paid for it too. The cart had dropped them on the other side of London Bridge and now Moss was feeling her way across the shingle, as though in a dream. In front of her, the sweep of the river was a thick soup of broken ice.

'Meltwater,' said Salter. 'Freeze is over. Good job too. Now we can all get back to makin a proper livin.'

Outside the shack Salter lit a fire and turned his back while Moss took off her dress to dry, handing her a sack to wrap round her shivering body. Then they sat, huddled together, while the fire pit crackled.

'*You* are one crazy coloppe of a shore girl,' said Salter. 'Wanderin off by yerself.'

The cheer in Salter's voice tugged Moss back from her bleak thoughts.

'How did you know where I was?' she asked.

'I guessed you might be headin off fer Hampton,' said Salter. 'A word with Eel-Eye Jack and me farthins bought some sharp pairs of eyes.'

'Eyes?'

'Scouts on the river. Paid fair and square to check where you'd gone.'

'You used your money to find me?'

'Can't think why.'

He was teasing her. She almost managed a smile.

'I mean,' said Salter, 'I'd got so used to . . . well, livin by meself. An' when you left that night on top of Farringdon Hill I thought things would just go back to the way they was, before you turned up.' He scratched his head underneath the tousle of hair.

'But when I got back, I dunno . . . they just didn't.'

Moss blinked.

Just as the fire warmed her body, having him next to her now warmed her inside. And she wondered about Salter and whether his thieving and cheating didn't matter so much after all. Was this friendship? She didn't know. Because a friend was something she'd never had.

'Yer dad was on the shore,' said Salter.

'Pa?'

Salter nodded.

'How do you know it was him?'

'Askin everyone he could about a tangle-haired girl, bout yer age, answers to the name of Moss, can't swim, stubborn as a Cheapside mule.'

'He said that?'

'Not the last bit.'

'Oh.'

'Anyway, it was yer pa, all right.'

'Did he come here? Did you speak to him?'

Salter nodded. 'I didn't say nothin much. Said

I seen a girl like he was describin, but you'd passed through and I didn't know where you'd gone.'

'And . . . how . . . how did he seem to you?'

'Like he was eaten up with so much worry, you'd have thought a barn full of rats had been gnawin at the poor fella.'

'Oh!' said Moss. 'I didn't . . . I mean, when I left I –'

She turned away from Salter, swallowing the guilt that welled in her throat. *Everything I've done, I did for you.* For the second time that night, she felt fingers of ice reach inside to clutch her heart. Somewhere out on the river, a trickle of laughter mixed with the lap of the waves.

'So,' said Salter. 'Hitchin a lift on the Queen's sleigh. That takes some nerve!'

'It was going to Hampton.'

'And what's so special about Hampton?'

'It was where my mother died. And where –' Moss hesitated. She wanted to tell Salter about the Riverwitch, but he'd never believe her. Anyway, even

279

if he did, what good would it do now? In two days she'd be twelve and the Witch would be coming for her. She needed time to think. She needed a plan.

She patted her dress. It was almost dry. She carried it behind the shack and pulled it on over her head.

Out of the light of the fire, her eyes adjusted to the dark. In the distance she could make out the vague outline of a figure, hunched under the low moon. The figure was walking slowly. It held something glowing. A burning torch or a lantern perhaps. Then it stopped and made its way towards one of the little huts that clung to the muddy banks. Moss watched as the hunched figure bent down, as though trying to look through the cracks in the rough wood walls.

'Salter . . .' whispered Moss.

The figure was approaching Salter's shack now. She could hear its footsteps, slow and deliberate, like the careful tread of a bird. And the scrape of a swinging lantern.

'Salter,' whispered Moss again, 'don't ask me why, just do as I say.'

'Eh?'

'Quick! Away from the fire!' she hissed, pulling him behind the shack. She kicked over a large fish crate and shoved Salter under, tucking herself in next to him before pulling the crate over their heads.

'Leatherboots, what are you playin at?' said Salter.

'Just keep quiet and don't move.'

The shingle crunched.

'You hear it?'

'I hear it.'

'Don't even breathe.'

They listened to the sound of feet picking their way across the shingle.

Through a crack in the crate, Moss saw an arc of orange light split the darkness. Behind it, the figure was close now. She could see it stooping, back bent like a shepherd's crook.

It was the ragged man.

The figure walked right up to Salter's shack

and stopped outside the tiny window.

Huddled under the crate, they watched as he held the lantern to the window and peered inside. The shack lit up as the orange beam licked its way in, picking through the dark corners.

'What –' whispered Salter. Moss put her finger to her lips.

The ragged man was looking for something. But whatever it was, he didn't find it in Salter's shack. The lantern creaked. Now he was walking towards them. Moss felt every hair on her body stiffen as his footsteps crunched past the crate. She held her breath. The footsteps passed, then grew fainter.

When Moss was sure she could hear them no longer, they crawled out from under the crate. Again, she put her fingers to her lips and squinted into the darkness. The orange lantern swayed, making its way up the shore towards the fishermen's huts.

'Who *was* that?' said Salter.

But Moss had set off nimbly over the shingle, taking a line away from the water's edge, in the direction of the swinging lantern. By the time Salter caught up with her, she was crouching in the shadow of Belinsgate Wharf.

'Leatherboots, what are you doin?' hissed Salter.

'That man,' whispered Moss. 'I've seen him before.'

'Who is he then?'

'I don't know exactly. I've never seen his face. I don't know his name. He was in the Tower. The soldiers carried a sack for him. And there was a hand –'

'What d'you mean, *a hand?*'

'In the sack by the Bloody Tower. And then I saw him again. Out here on the shore.'

'I've no idea what yer on about, Leatherboots, but sure as a dog likes to lick its own bum, that ragged devil ain't up to no good. An' if he ever shows up near my shack again, he'll be sorry he did. Ain't just sprats I can gut with that knife of mine.'

'Salter. Look.'

A small shape crawled out of one of the fishermen's huts. It was a young boy. Bleary with sleep, he tottered to his feet and stumbled a few steps away from his home.

Salter stifled a laugh. 'If you got to go, you got to go,' he said.

'Shhh!' said Moss. She was looking around for the glow of the orange lantern, but it had vanished. They watched the boy fumble with his garment, then heard the spatter of wee on the shingle.

There was a movement behind the hut. Small. Just the flick of a shadow. But Moss saw it.

'There!' she whispered.

'Where?'

The boy had finished and began to tidy himself. He rubbed his eyes, still half asleep. Slowly, from behind the boy, out of the darkness reached a hand. Curled and ready to grasp. A claw in the dark.

'Aahhgghhh!' Moss sprang forward. 'Get away from him!' she screamed.

The hand snapped back into the darkness.

Skidding on the shingle, Moss raced past the boy and round the back of the hut.

There was no one there.

The boy was wide-eyed in shock. He sat down on the pebbles and began to cry. The door of his hut burst open and a candle poked out, followed by an angry face.

'What's all this? Topper! Get back in here! Right now, yer little flounder!'

The boy sniffed his way back inside the hut, taking a clout on the ear on the way. His father stepped out of the hut and held the candle aloft.

'Who's there? Come out, whoever you are!'

Moss stepped into the candlelight.

The father looked her up and down, then called back over his shoulder. 'It's all right, Bess, it's only a girl!'

'Well, thank the saints for that! For a minute I thought –'

'Never mind that! Just get the boy back to bed!' The man turned to Moss. 'Now *you*, get back to yer own hut. You've no business skulkin around the foreshore at night. Ain't a safe place to go wanderin.'

'Please,' said Moss, 'behind your hut – there was someone. A man –'

'A man?' The father took a few steps beyond the hut and shone the candle into the darkness. 'Well there ain't no one there now,' he said. 'Off you go.' He stomped back inside and slammed the door.

Moss turned to Salter. 'Well, don't go out of your way to help me or anything! At least you could have backed me up.'

Salter shrugged. 'He wouldn't have listened to me any more than he listened to you. It's the middle of the night. These fishermen are tired. They don't want to be launchin a search for no invisible man.'

'Wait,' said Moss. She walked a little way from the hut, then bent down, raking the darkness above the shingle with her arms.

'Leatherboots, have you gone mad as a rabbit?'

'No.' Her hand clanged against metal. 'Here!'

She strode back to Salter and lifted a heavy object in front of his face. 'Look! His lantern! He must have dropped it when he ran away.' She looked out towards the river. 'It *was* him.'

'Who's him? What are you talkin about?'

'The ragged man. I told you, I've seen him in the Tower. He comes at night with a lantern.'

'Eh?'

'He comes looking, here on the riverbank. In the fishermen's huts. In your shack.'

'Lookin' fer what?'

'I think . . .' Moss's voice shrank to a whisper. 'I think he's looking for *children*.'

'Children?'

'Salter, I think . . . *he* is the snatcher.'

'You what?'

'The one who's taking children from the shore.'

'Let me get this straight. Yer tellin me there's a crooked man from the Tower of London an' he comes out here and is takin children? But what for?'

'I don't know.'

Moss dredged her memory for every encounter with that ragged man. The bent figure stalking the shore at night. The man the soldiers had been afraid of by the Bloody Tower, who came and went like a ghost. She remembered the very first time she'd seen him, under the wharf, near the tunnel entrance. Was *he* using the tunnel too? To come and go undetected, to seek out children at night on the shore? She thought back to that day under the wharf, where she'd noticed the small boat, and in it a lantern and a sack.

Moss gasped. Was the boat *his*? That night at Traitors' Gate, he'd arrived by boat. And the day of the Abbot's execution she'd been spooked by a boat in the mist, by the sound of whimpering out on the river, the splash and churning of the water. And then the strange trail of ice, studded with coins . . .

'Salter,' she said, 'I think that he's taking children from the bank. Taking them to the Tower. Then the next day he rows them out on to the river. And then, I don't know, he gets money . . .'

She could almost feel the claw-like grip on her throat. The choking smell of char and burn. What had he said? *Not yet for you, but soon enough . . .*

Something clicked inside Moss's head.

'*He will find you,*' she whispered to herself. The words of the Riverwitch. What if *He* was the ragged man?

Fear crawled up her spine. It gripped her throat, stopped her mouth. She sank down to her knees on the shingle.

The ragged man.

The ragged man was coming for her.

CHAPTER TWENTY-TWO
Ghosts in the Walls

Salter wasn't keen at all. It had taken most of the day and all Moss's powers of persuasion to get him as far as Tower Wharf.

'This is where I stop, Leatherboots. I ain't goin in no tunnel. I ain't no mole, burrowin in the ground. I ain't goin nowhere I can't see the sky.'

'It's just a tunnel.' But even as she spoke those words, the thought of the ragged man who might be hiding in there somewhere filled her with dread.

'An' that ain't all,' said Salter, jabbing a thumb at

the Tower walls. 'That place spooks me. There ain't nothin you can do to drag me in there. Even if you showed me a thousand tunnels an' all of them were lined with red velvet, paved with gold sovereigns an' filled with every roast chicken in the city.'

Moss blinked at the weirdness of this picture. But she kept walking.

'And,' continued Salter, 'if *you've* got any sense, you'll stay out of there too.'

'I just need to see my pa. Anyway, I'll be fine.' She sounded more confident than she felt.

'You don't know that,' said Salter. 'You say that ragged devil is comin and goin. In an' out of that tunnel. Takin his sack and fillin it and then rowin it through Traitors' Gate. Well, *I* say that's reason enough to steer clear of the place.'

'I'll be careful. He won't see me. I know all the hiding places.'

'I'm just sayin. You just don't know what yer gettin yerself into, Leatherboots. An' if you've got a mousefart's-worth of sense, you'll stay well out of it.'

She knew Salter was right. She hadn't told him that the ragged man was looking for her. That was even more reason to stay away from the Tower. But tomorrow she'd be twelve. No matter what might happen, she had to see Pa.

'Leatherboots?'

'I hear you.'

But she'd made up her mind. She'd go in just before curfew, under cover of darkness. Less chance she'd be spotted going in and out of the garderobe drop. She'd sneak to the forge, see Pa, then head straight back out before high tide flooded the tunnel. Then she'd get as far away from the river as possible. Maybe she could find a place where there were no rivers. Did such a place exist? And the ragged man? Well, she'd just have to take her chances.

'Well, here's what *I* think,' said Salter. 'There's brave an' there's stupid an' I know which one *I* am.'

By the time they got to Tower Wharf, the river was soaking up the last rays of a cold winter sun.

Moss led Salter to the hole, wading through the incoming tide.

'This is it,' said Moss. 'Help me, will you?'

They unblocked the hole together. Salter peered into the blackness.

'You sure you won't come?' said Moss.

Salter shook his head.

'Pile the stones back up when I'm in. I'll be back before the tide turns.'

'I'll be waitin right here.'

Moss stepped into the tunnel and began wading as silently as possible, in case the ragged man should be coming the other way. She could hear Salter cursing his head off as he tried to clunk the stones back into the hole and she wished she'd told him to be quiet. His mutterings filled the tunnel, but they made her heart glad. And she smiled to think how shocked she'd been at his foul language, when now it seemed as normal as the sound of waves.

She reached the end of the tunnel and stopped. There was no sign of the ragged man. Her feet found the slippery footholds up to the garderobe drop. She climbed to the top and hauled herself through the gap, gagging on the familiar stench. She slipped through the door and into the bustling yard.

It felt like she'd been away from this place a thousand years. Everything about her life had changed. *She* had changed. And she knew that whatever happened now, she couldn't go back to this.

Moss walked under the arch to the Bloody Tower. Half expecting the ragged man to be waiting in the shadows, she hurried on. She would find Pa. Tell him everything. Tell him . . . goodbye.

The door of the forge was closed. Moss pushed at it gently.

'Pa?'

It was dark inside. And cold. The fire was out.

Moss crept into the room. She checked Pa's pallet. Empty. On the table were the remains of a loaf of bread. She picked it up. Rock hard. She put her nose in the jug next to it. Sour milk. Had he stopped eating and drinking?

In the corner was the kindling box. Moss gathered an armful of sticks and laid them, criss-cross, in the fire bed. After several visits to the woodpile and some vigorous bellow-pumping, she had a good blaze going. There was water in the bucket. She poured it into the cooking pot, along with the bread and an onion, and hung the pot from its hook over the fire. At least there'd be soup for Pa when he returned.

She waited, alone, by the crackling fire. But Pa did not come.

The soup, ready long ago, sat cold on the table. The grey sky turned to dusk. Still he did not come.

Was he out there somewhere? Walking the river? The streets of the city? What if he never came back to the forge? Moss jumped up. She *had* to see him. Time was slipping away. She had until midnight. Her birthday. She'd just have to go out there and find him.

It was well past curfew as Moss slunk back across Tower Green. Over the South Wall she could hear the slop of waves against stone. She'd have to be quick. The tunnel would soon be flooded by the tide.

Through the arch of the Bloody Tower, across the yard, sticking to the shadows of the high wall, she made her way to the garderobe drop. But when she got there, something made her stop and turn.

Footsteps. Under the arch of the Bloody Tower. Followed by the gruff voices of soldiers. She ducked below the steps and peeped out. Two soldiers were standing at Traitors' Gate, the same soldiers she'd seen there before.

'Ned,' whispered one, 'I don't know how much longer I can go on with this.'

'Gawd, give me strength!'

'He's still crawlin an' hissin through me dreams, Ned. I mean, we saw him die, didn't we? On that burnin pile of faggots. An' now he's back an' –'

'Quiet, Laces. Devil help us, we takes his money, we does his business and we keeps our traps shut.'

'But –'

'Listen, whether he's back from the dead or devil knows where, *you* shouldn't ask so many questions. Take his money, Laces, and thank yer lucky breeches he only comes after you in yer dreams.'

'I –'

'Just be ready to grab that sack.'

They fell silent and now Moss heard the gate creaking open and the thunk of a boat as it nudged its way in.

Up the steps of Traitors' Gate came the ragged man, his hood shrouding his face as always.

'Sack's in the boat,' he hissed. 'Be quick about it. This one's coming round. A skulker from under the wharf.'

Just as before, the man opened his pouch and Moss heard coins chink into the waiting hands of the soldiers.

She watched the soldiers drag the sack to the top of the steps then hump it across the yard to the Bloody Tower. The ragged man shuffled after them.

Over the South Wall, the scrunch of waves on shingle was getting louder. Salter would be waiting. If she didn't go now, all chance of making it out of the Tower on this tide would be lost. She had to find Pa. In just a few hours she would be twelve. And then what? If she was right, that ragged man would be coming for her. By midnight, she wanted to be as far away from him and the river as possible.

The door of the Bloody Tower clanged shut.

Moss felt the sickness rise in her throat. The sack. Inside that sack . . . She didn't want to think about it. Where were they taking it? Her heart was thudding a hole in her chest.

Leave it . . . She *couldn't* leave it. Inside that sack was a child.

Quickly, she crept back along the base of the wall. Under the arch she took off her boots and stashed them behind a barrel. Bare feet. Nimble feet. Now she could run as quiet as a mouse.

Pushing open the door to the Bloody Tower, she slid in. The narrow passage flickered with light from a distant torch. Moss swallowed. Like most of the Tower folk, she'd always given the Bloody Tower a wide berth. Its rooms and passageways were haunted. That's what Nell had told her. Two princes had been murdered here. In their beds one night. Their bodies were never found. Nell said their screams could still be heard in the walls.

Moss listened now. Just the faint echo of footsteps coming from a shaft of steps to her left.

Her feet patted softly down the stone steps. She could hear the grunts of the soldiers. She followed them. Where were they going? The steps were taking her deep down, where the air was thick and fusty. She could feel the dank slime against her fingers as they brushed the wall. At the bottom of the steps, the corridor stretched in two directions. The tiniest ripple of torchlight fluttered on the wall far ahead. Moss padded after it. Once or twice she lost sight of the torchlight, feeling her away along blind twists and turns. These passageways were unknown to her, deep in the bowels of the Bloody Tower, their skin peeling and their breath rotten. Moss could well believe these walls might whisper their secrets to those who disturbed them.

Now the voices of the soldiers were louder. Moss slowed her pace. There was a blaze of light at the end of the passage. She edged closer, her bare feet making no sound on the stone floor.

She stopped behind a doorway. Through it was a room, flickering like a fireplace in the torchlight. The ragged man was nowhere to be seen. The room was empty save for the two soldiers, the sack they carried and, in one corner, a large iron cage. Moss watched the soldiers dump the sack on the ground.

'He ain't movin, Ned. That ragged feller must have given him quite a bash on his head.'

The soldier grunted.

'And what does he want them for anyway?'

'Why are you askin me? Sells em to slavers for all I know.'

The soldiers began kicking and rolling the sack

towards the cage. The bundle was lifeless at first, but their kicks seemed to waken it. Two wiry arms shot from the neck of the sack and suddenly a head jerked free.

'Great Harry's piles! Get yer dirty great hooves off me!'

Moss knew that voice. She stumbled back against the wall.

'Salter . . .?' she whispered.

One of the soldiers whipped round. 'Did you hear that?'

But the other soldier was busy stuffing Salter's arms back in the sack. 'Quiet, yer foul-mouthed little rat!' He clamped a hand to Salter's mouth.

'Ned – did you hear that noise?'

'Put a lid on it, Laces! You're jumpy as a cat on coals.'

'A noise, Ned. *In the walls.*'

'Eh?'

Laces looked anxiously over his shoulder. Moss crept a little closer, taking care to stay in the shadow of the door frame. Laces was still looking about, as though he expected something to jump out of the walls at any moment.

'Ned, it sounded like a child.'

Moss got it. The soldier thought her whisper was a ghost. One of the murdered princes maybe . . .

Why not? She could be a voice in the walls.

'*Help . . . us,*' she whispered.

'Ned.'

'*Help us . . .*' Her thin voice echoed round the passageway.

'Ned, did you hear that?'

'I heard it.'

By now both soldiers had let go of the sack and Moss saw that Salter was working his arms free once again.

'*Two boys,*' she whispered, '*with knives in our backs.*'

'Ned!' cried Laces. 'It's them princes!'

'*You disturb us. You tread on our souls. Leave us!*'

The soldiers began edging out of the room, but before they'd got to the doorway Moss felt a sudden, crippling pain in her shoulder, as though she had been gripped by the talons of a bird. She was shoved through the doorway, where she fell to her knees.

A voice hissed behind her. 'Here's your ghost!'

Moss staggered to her feet and looked up.

Into the room stepped the ragged man. As his face found the flickering light, Moss gasped.

Strapped to his head was a mask of parched leather that covered almost half his face from the jawline up, with roughly cut holes for his nostrils and mouth. Where the light caught the exposed skin, it was strangely blackened, split like dry earth, and would have seemed lifeless were it not for his eyes, two specks of jet, darting this way and that.

'A little sneaker, eh? Prying and spying and all alone in the darkness of the Bloody Tower.' The ragged man snapped his hand at the soldiers. 'You two! Get the boy into the cage!'

He turned his gaze back to Moss. 'I have been looking for you these past days. But here you are, delivered into my hands in a pretty twist of fate.'

The soldiers were dragging Salter, pummelling and kicking, across the room.

'GET OFF ME, YER COWARDS!' he yelled. 'YOU'VE GOT LESS GUTS THAN A PAN OF COCKLES!'

'Shut it, yer little rat, or we'll knock yer teeth out!'

'Let him go!' cried Moss. She sprang forward, pouncing on the back of one soldier, until the clawed grip of the ragged man tore her off. He held her fast.

'Let him go! He's done nothing to you!'

'How touching.' The ragged man bent down, his face close to hers, and Moss found herself choking on a smell like smoke. 'But put away your brave face, little sneaker. His fate is sealed. As is yours. Into the cage with both of them!'

Moss and Salter were thrust into the iron cage. The soldiers banged the door shut and held it while the ragged man locked it with a key that hung from a chain on his belt.

'You may go now.' The ragged man waved the soldiers out of the room. 'Come back at dawn. I will take out the boy on the next high tide. The girl . . . she will follow.'

The room was quiet, save for the rattling breaths of the ragged man.

'What do you want from us, yer ragged devil?' said Salter.

'It's not what *I* want,' he hissed, 'it's what *she* wants.'

'She? Who?'

The ragged man lifted a torch from a wall-bracket and walked slowly towards the cage. The pouch of coins hung heavy from his belt, *chink-chinking* as he went.

'Well, *that* is quite a story. But since you're not going anywhere . . .' He lowered the torch and pushed it through the bars. Salter recoiled.

'Tell me, foul-mouthed boy. Have you ever seen a man burn?'

'No I ain't.'

'Put your hand in the flame,' the ragged man said.

'Yeah, right. Go take a runnin jump into a pit of pig snot!'

For someone whose body seemed so broken, he was quick. The ragged man whipped his hand into the cage and grabbed Salter's wrist, thrusting it into the fire. Salter screamed. Moss punched out through the bars and the torch dropped to the ground. The ragged man cackled and his chest rattled like a box of bones. He picked up the torch. Then he raised his own hand. Moss could see his skin, scaly and hard as a crow's leg. Slowly he drew the hand into the centre of the burning torch. It flared and crackled. Moss gasped.

'You might think,' he hissed, 'that a man who'd been burned to within an inch of his life would be afraid of fire? Not so.'

Moss forced herself to look at him. 'You were . . . burned?'

He licked his parched lips. Then slowly, he undid the strap at the back of his mask. It dropped to the floor. The face of the ragged man was as cracked and blackened as his hands.

'A priest I was,' he said. 'A man of God. Here in the chapel of this Tower.' He laughed a brittle laugh. 'But temptation came my way and I stole. I took what I could, when I could. From the altar, from the crypt, from the bodies buried there. It was too easy. No one suspects a priest.' His jet eyes flicked this way and that. 'But I was not the only thief. Two soldiers, as greedy as I. The soldiers you saw here tonight. Men who know where a cross or a goblet or a gold chain can fetch a price and no questions asked. But then came the day the soldiers turned on me and I was caught.'

He paused and his rasping breath filled the room. Moss glanced across at Salter nursing his hand, horror and revulsion on his face.

The ragged man continued. 'I was taken from the Tower by soldiers. The two who betrayed me were among them, pretending they knew nothing. They set my broken body on a pile of burning faggots.

Gawped and jeered as the flames charred my skin. Drank in the smell of a roasting man, lapped up my pain. Such pain – like a thousand knives driven into my eyes.' He drew a breath. 'They thought I was dead. They left me there. But rain came. The fire hissed and spat and became smoke. And I cursed my betrayers and crawled from that smouldering fire into the river, where I willed the water to take away my pain or take me instead.'

The ragged man sat back, his body creaking as he leant against the wall.

'That day in the river, I called for help. But who would help me? Who would come?'

Moss's words were a whisper in the torchlight. 'The Riverwitch . . .'

'Yes. The Riverwitch.' A smile split the ragged man's lips. 'How lucky I was. A bargain was struck that day. She would take away my pain. In return I would salve hers.'

'Salve her pain? By snatching children?' said Moss. 'By giving them to the Riverwitch?'

The ragged man unfurled a blackened hand.

'There was one in particular. The one born in water. *You*, little sneaker. The Executioner's daughter. I was to find *you*. And when the time came, bring you back to the river.'

Moss could not move. His words numbed her body. She watched, helpless, as the ragged man reached his hand inside the cage and grazed the stub of his finger across her cheek.

'So I came back to the Tower where I could keep an eye on you. And it suits my purpose well. Here, in the Bloody Tower, where it is deep and dark and the cry of a child is a ghost in the walls. I bring them in like rabbits in a sack, to await my river mistress who comes on the next high tide.'

'Sweet Mary an' the devil's bones,' whispered Salter.

'A thief I was,' said the ragged man. 'A thief who was made a devil. A wicked deed that spawned a deed far worse, then another.'

'But where will it end?' said Moss. '*You* could end it.'

'Ha!' said the ragged man. 'Why would I? I feel no pain. I am paid in gold for the work I do.' He put a hand to the pouch at his side and cackled. 'Riches from the river deep! I am a thief no more.'

He heaved himself to his feet and Moss heard his bones crack. 'Take what sleep you can, little sneaker. Know it shall be your last.'

He shuffled out of the cell, followed by his own flickering shadow. They heard his footsteps in the corridor, his cackle echoing back through the darkness.

'The one born in water . . . She belongs to the Riverwitch.'

CHAPTER TWENTY-THREE
A Trick

All night, Moss and Salter tried to free themselves from the cage. Rattling, pounding, kicking, scratching at the lock with their bare nails.

'Ain't it about time you told me exactly what's goin on?' said Salter while they worked. So Moss did. Told him about the Riverwitch. And about Pa's promise.

When she'd finished, Salter shook his head.

'Why keep all this to yerself, Leatherboots? Why didn't you just tell me?'

'Because . . .' Moss thought back to those first days with Salter. The newness. The freedom of no one really knowing who she was or where she'd come from. Living each day without Pa's anxious eyes on her back.

'Because,' she said, 'with you, I could just be myself.'

Salter shook the cage. 'Argghh! This thing is strong enough to hold a bear!' He slumped back against the bars. 'Well, I'll tell you one thing. We ain't breakin out tonight.'

Moss drew her knees tight to her chest and felt something move in her pocket. She stuck her hand in.

'Ow!' She pulled it out quickly. A spot of blood welled on the tip of her finger.

Carefully, she eased Queen Anne's silver bird out of her pocket. The two of them examined the tiny ornament.

'Well, it ain't no knife,' said Salter. 'I can't see us fightin our way out with *that*.'

'Wait though,' said Moss. She pushed the tiny beak into the lock on the cage and jiggled.

Salter grinned. 'Somewhere in that stubborn head of yours, there's a brain.'

He watched while she fiddled with the lock, scratching away, picking at the hole, wiggling the tiny beak every way. The lock held fast.

'Cussin lock!' Salter gave it a whack. 'Where's the luck when you need it?'

Moss put the bird back in her pocket. 'How long until dawn do you think?'

'Not long,' said Salter. 'I'll tell you one thing though. I'll be glad to get out of this devil's hole. I just want to see the river again.'

At dawn, the ragged man returned with the soldiers. He stood in front of the cage.

'The boy I will take to the bridge first. The girl . . . on the next tide.'

The ragged man unhooked the key from his robe

and Moss saw it, polished iron that glinted in the torchlight as he unlocked the cage. He rehung it on the chain and stood back as a soldier pulled Salter out, pinning his arms behind his back.

'Don't give us any trouble, you –' said the soldier. But he never got to finish his sentence. Salter's fist had taken out two of his front teeth. The soldier yelled and clamped his hand to his bleeding mouth. Salter sprang a kick, high and strong against the concave chest of the ragged man, sending him clattering back against the cage. There was a crack of bones.

The ragged man laughed, but quick as a dart he shot out an arm and grabbed Salter. He turned to the soldier. 'Stop whining and hold the boy.'

The soldier spat a gobbet of blood at Salter's face, seized both his arms and wrenched them once more behind his back. And while this was going on, Moss found herself looking at something else.

Dangling next to the bars of the cage was the key. Hooked to the chain on the ragged man's robe. Inches from her nose. It wouldn't take much. Just something to put in its place . . .

Her hand went to her pocket.

'Arghh!' Salter was struggling as the soldier pulled his arms tight. She heard a thud, then Salter was quiet.

Moss cupped the silver bird in her hand, feeling its weight. It was hard to tell. It might work. Slowly, she drew it out of her pocket. The ragged man still had his back to the cage.

Moss reached forward. Her fingertips touched the key, easing it off its hook. Slowly, with the other hand, she lifted the little bird, looping its clasped talons over the end of the hook. The little bird dangled upside down on the chain. Biting her lip, she watched the soldiers drag Salter out of the door. The ragged man followed, his head raised slightly.

In the doorway he stopped. 'Say goodbye to your friend, little sneaker,' he said. 'Nothing can save him now.'

Moss watched him go. Her mouth was dry. In her hand was the key.

CHAPTER TWENTY-FOUR
Drowning

As soon as the passageway was quiet, Moss fumbled the cage door open and crawled out. Then she ran. Blindly, down the passageway, scraping her elbows on the walls, feeling her way through the pitch-black, until she came at last to the shaft of steps. She scrambled to the top and heaved open the door to the Bloody Tower.

She could hear the waves, high against the wall. The tide was in. The tunnel would be flooded. How would she get out now? She could feel her heart pumping, jagged beats that leapt from her chest.

The gates! She wasn't a prisoner. She could go through the gates!

Moss sprinted down the yard, past the Bell Tower, past the garderobe drop, to the gatehouse. A Yeoman stood stiffly in front of the lowered portcullis. He looked her up and down.

'And what do you want? Get out of it!'

'I want to . . . to go out, please?'

The Yeoman chortled. 'What? You think we'd lift the portcullis for a scrag-end of a basket girl? Just because she turns up at the gates?'

'But –'

'NO BUTS! Off you go before I whip the soles of those bare feet!'

Moss backed away from the gatehouse.

The Tower was waking up. Windows were opening and she heard the whinny of a horse from the stables.

She ran back to the yard. There was no time. She had to go now. *Now.* Or Salter would be gone. And if she couldn't get through the gate, she knew of only one other way out of the Tower. The thought of it almost made her cry out in fear.

Moss scrambled down the steps and burst into the garderobe drop. It didn't matter who heard her. By the time they figured out what was happening, it would be too late. And where she was going, no one would follow.

By the hole in the garderobe wall she could hear the slop of water below. Her chest lurched. She slithered down the well and caught a foothold just above the water.

The tunnel was completely flooded.

Moss knew there was no way she could hold her breath from one end of the tunnel to the other. All she could hope was to find a pocket of air somewhere. Some little nook the river hadn't managed to fill. If she couldn't . . . Moss wrenched her head from that terrible thought and dropped into the water.

The cold was nothing. She almost wished it was

colder. A distraction from the horror pounding in her head. She breathed in and out, gasping lungfuls of air. Then she heaved her chest up, drawing the biggest breath she could manage, and ducked into the tunnel.

All around was green-black. Her eyes open, she could see nothing but the dead space of water.

Count, she told herself. Fifty paces to the end. *One, two . . .*

Clawing the side of the tunnel with one hand, she moved forward, trying to keep her feet on the bottom. With her other hand she groped for the ceiling, pushing herself down so her body wouldn't tip. If she stumbled, if for one moment she lost her bearings, she was finished.

Eleven, twelve, thirteen . . .

Against her ears, the noise of the water was deafening. A river too wild to be trapped in a tunnel. She could feel it bucking against the walls, trying to push her over.

Twenty-one, twenty-two . . .

She wished now for her boots. Something to weigh down her feet. To make her solid against the angry crush of water.

Twenty-nine . . .

She wanted to breathe. She imagined the cold water all around her was air. Clean, bright air.

Just one breath. Her chest began to spasm. *Just one . . .* She forced the feeling deep inside until her lungs burned with the effort.

Thirty? Thirty-five? How many? How many paces? She'd lost count.

Breathe. No! Now she pressed her mouth to the ceiling, hoping for any scrap of air. The rocks tore her face. She forced her legs onwards. The water swirled around her, pulling her, dragging her. She had to breathe. *Don't breathe!* She had to.

Moss's helpless lungs drew breath. Instantly she choked. Gulps of riverwater blocked her throat. Her legs thrashed in the blackness. Her lungs were burning now, tight and useless. Her body writhed against the walls of the tunnel. The blackness closed in. She pressed her face against the jagged rock.

And there it was. The tiniest chink of air. Drawn in. Spluttered out. Coughed in again. Breathed. Hard. Short, torn gasps. Until she was dizzy. Air.

She turned her head, crushed her cheek against the ceiling as hard as she could to keep her lips above the water. She must be near the end. *Do it*, she told herself. *Now*.

She heaved a huge lungful of air into her chest and ducked back into the flooded tunnel, striding as hard as she could against the heaving tide water. Three paces and she struck hard rock. Above her the roof had disappeared. She scrabbled upwards, feeling for the loose stones that blocked the hole. With a strength she would not have believed possible, she kicked and pushed at the stones until she felt them fall away. She fought her way through the hole and was sucked out by the current, dragging her up to the surface.

'Ow!' Her head struck the underside of the wharf. Then the current whipped her from below and suddenly she was out in the open river.

Crash! Her body was thrown against the wharf wall. She grabbed at a piece of floating wood and let the suck of the river pull her along, past the wooden bellies of huge ships that knocked against the wharf. Then a wave washed over her head, dragging her under and tumbling her to the bank.

She would have stayed there, flat on her back, just drinking in the sky. But the thrill of surviving the tunnel was knocked back by the fear of what might be happening now. To Salter. Out on the river.

Her breath came in snatches as she tore across the shingle to Salter's shack. What she was about to do was foolish and reckless. She should run as far away from the river as she could. Far from any river. But she knew she could not. Somewhere out there was Salter. And if she didn't save him, no one would.

Salter's boat was just where he'd left it the day before. She began dragging it across the shingle, then remembered. The axe.

She ran back to the shack. Her hands shook as she threw crates aside, scrabbling down into the hole she'd made in the shingle. The axe was still there. Grabbing it, she raced back to the boat, threw in the axe, pushed off from the water's edge and leapt in.

The bridge. That was what the ragged man had said. He was taking Salter to London Bridge. She could just make it out, a looming shadow through the fog that hung around her in a greasy cloud.

The river was millpond calm. Moss took up the oars and struggled, trying to dip and pull through the water, as she'd seen Salter do many times. He'd made it look easy. After several minutes of frustrated splashing, she threw down one oar and knelt, face forward, paddling a two-handed stroke, first one side of the boat, then the other, and in this way she glided slowly through the fog, glad she couldn't see what might be coming from below.

A child that is born to the river shall return to the river. She'd fought it, defied it, but the Riverwitch's prophecy had come true. Here she was. On the very morning of her twelfth birthday. In a tiny boat. On the river. She tried to swallow the panic that welled within. The only thing that mattered was getting to that bridge.

Out of the fog it loomed, sudden and massive. Moss steered the boat to rest against one of the thick stone columns.

A cackle echoed round the arches. *The ragged man.* She heard the chink of a hammer. Where was he?

Moss grabbed the chain at the base of the arch and slipped silently round it, pulling the boat as she went. Then she paddled to the next arch and stopped.

Through the mist echoed the sound of a tinkling bell. She knew she didn't have much time. Fighting the urge to paddle away as fast as she could, Moss waited until she saw a pointed shape poke through the fog. She watched the thin, bent figure glide through the murk. His breath rattled in his chest, but his laughter seemed to come from somewhere else. Somewhere between the living and the dead.

When she was sure he had gone, Moss took up her oar. As quickly as she was able, she paddled, whispering.

'Salter?'

There was no reply. So she called softly, not trusting the fog that swirled round her. 'Salter? Are you there?'

Silence. She tried again. A little louder. 'Salter! It's me!'

Nothing, just the lapping of water dulled by the fog.

'Salter!' Moss could feel desperation closing in, trying to drag her down. But she paddled on. Then a faint noise. A cough. The clinking of metal.

'Salter? Where are you?'

'Leatherboots, is that you?' His voice croaked in the mist.

Her boat clattered against a stone column and there he was, crouching on a thin ledge. His leg was shackled by a long chain, tethered to the stone.

'Salter! It's me, it's me!' Moss nearly capsized. 'It's me!'

'Are you *completely* nuts?' said Salter. 'Comin out here on yer own.'

'Are you all right? Are you hurt?'

'Bumped and bruised, that's all.' Moss was scrambling for the chain, looping the boat rope through it. 'Listen, I don't know what you think yer doin, but you'd better turn round right now an' get back to the bank. That ragged devil's chained me up good to this bridge an' there ain't no way your scrawny arms is goin to break metal. So go on. Get out of here. While yer still can, Leatherboots.'

'No, Salter. Look!' She held up the axe.

'Harry's hairy armpits! Where did you get that?'

'Doesn't matter.' She wobbled to the edge of the boat. 'Keep your leg as far away as possible.'

'Yer not goin' to –'

'Stand back!'

Moss swung the axe and brought it down hard against the chain.

'Holy coloppes!' cried Salter.

Moss swung again and the axe clanged against

326

the stone, sparks flying from the rusty steel. The chain did not break. She whacked it again. And again, sparks fizzing in the mist. Still the chain did not break. Moss gripped the axe tight.

'Arghh!' She brought it down with all the strength she could find and, with a blow that almost snapped the axehead from the handle, the chain finally smashed in two.

Moss flung down the axe. 'Come on!' she cried, grabbing Salter's arm. He leapt in, landing on all fours, before steadying himself and the wobbling boat.

'I said it before and I'll say it again,' said Salter, 'yer one crazy idiot of a girl.' He pulled himself to his feet. 'But that ain't always a bad thing.'

Moss was panting and her hands were sore. For a moment she forgot all about the Riverwitch and the ragged man.

'Salter, whatever happens –'

'*Whatever happens?* What happens is we get the hell out of here. You found me and you saved me. I don't know how you did it or where you got that old axe, but it don't matter.'

'No,' said Moss, 'it doesn't matter.' She smiled at Salter and instantly he smiled back, eyes crinkling through his dirt-smudged cheeks.

That was the moment she knew. That they were friends. For sure.

'Come on, give me the oars,' yelled Salter. 'Let's go! Wait. What was that?'

Something was happening to the water.

'Do you feel that?' said Salter.

Moss nodded. The boat was shaking.

'What *is* that?'

Some sort of weird current was pulling them back, away from the bridge. Everything lurched. Moss and Salter were thrown on to all fours. The fog lifted and Moss could see tiny waves skittering across the water. The river was trembling like a living thing.

Then the trembling stopped.

The air was a thick silence. But through it came

something else. A rumbling. Like thunder. Like a thousand continuous thunderclaps.

Through the arches of the bridge, Moss saw a wide band of silver-white hovering over the river in the distance.

Something big. Powerful. Coming towards them.

And adrift in Salter's tiny boat, Moss knew there was nothing she could do to stop it.

CHAPTER TWENTY-FIVE
The Great Wave

A wave. A great curl of froth rising out of the water, two trees high. Moss barely had time to grip the sides of the boat before it crashed through the bridge, wrapping its fists round each arch, sending chunks of stone tumbling into the river. A wall of water that shattered the boat, ripping the sides clean off until it was little more than a raft. And all Moss could do was hang on as the churning water bowled her over and over, gasping and choking for air in the crush.

When she came up for air she was clinging to the raft. There was no sign of Salter.

'WHERE ARE YOU?' Her cry was trampled by the roar of the wave.

She felt herself pitch forwards, then up and up until the raft was hoisted high above the river like a platter of food. She hauled herself on to her stomach, trying to keep the raft steady, trying to point it in the direction of the tumbling foam. It took the strength of her whole body and she heard her own voice yelling against the noise, as if one small girl could match the bellow of a mighty wave.

The wave rolled on, thundering like a giant wheel.

Through the din she heard a cry. Scrambling in the wall of water, two arms flailed in and out of the surf, a head bobbing to the surface.

'SALTER!' Gripping the sides of the raft, she steered it into the wave, slicing across the surf. She almost cut into him, pulling up just in time to see his head go under.

'SALTER!' she screamed again, and with one

hand grabbed at the bobbing head, the other juddering with the force of the wave under the raft. She missed.

'SALTER!' Again he was buffeted under the surface and again she steered towards him. When his head came up it was inches from the raft. Moss lunged, almost losing her grip as she came up, holding Salter by the scruff of his neck. His hands groped for the planks and he clung to the side while Moss forced the raft back into the curl of the wave.

'Weepin leg wounds!' Salter's yell was snatched by the roar of the water.

'Just hold on!' screamed Moss.

As she struggled to keep them from pitching under, Salter dragged himself onboard until his body was flat next to hers.

The wave rolled on. Faster and faster. Ripping timber, bricks and bones from the river bed. Old things. Dead things. Dredged up and given new life in the tumbling wave.

Now the wave was growing, a curling wall of

water above them, its sides like thick green glass. And as Moss stared, transfixed, a dark shadow swam alongside. Through the rushing water Moss saw a tattered face, skin peeled back by the force of the wave.

'Look out!' yelled Moss. A thin, flat boat bowled towards them through the surf and the two rolled sideways, tipping the raft to one side, missing the boat by inches as it crashed past them.

The face vanished.

'Hold on, Leatherboots!'

Banks and houses flashed past as the wave rolled on, gobbling the river until the snaking line of silver widened to a vast plateau. Moss screamed as the wave tossed the pair of them, clinging to the raft, through the air, smacking them hard back down into the river. The force of their landing knocked the breath from Moss's chest. Salter was on his side, retching and spitting.

The water was calm.

Moss tried to swallow her panic. In front of Salter

333

she didn't want to show she was afraid.

'*What*, in the name of Harry's earholes, was *that*?' said Salter.

But before Moss could reply, the tail end of the raft dipped. Moss whipped round. Two charred hands were hauling themselves slowly aboard.

'Hello, little whelps.' The ragged man's face split into a smile. His mask was off and he licked the saltwater from his cracked face.

Salter threw himself to the stern and banged his fists down on the ragged man's hands.

'Get off, yer devil!' he yelled. 'You'll have us all over!'

But the man's fingers gripped the raft tight. 'Haven't you noticed? I don't die so easily. But how did you escape my cage I wonder, little sneaker?' His eyes drilled into Moss. 'No matter. It was all for nothing.' A fist shot out and landed a blow in Salter's face. Salter reeled back, clutching his eye. Slowly, the ragged man hauled himself aboard. His cloak was sodden. His bag of gold chinked against his side. And something flashed next to it. Something bright. The bird! Queen Anne's silver bird still hung where Moss had placed it, on the hook of the ragged man's belt.

Moss dived at the ragged man and the unexpected force of her lunge knocked him sideways. Twisting herself away from his flailing hands, she made a grab for the bird. She missed. Rolling away, she scrabbled on to all fours.

The ragged man regained his balance and looked at Moss with curiosity. Then down at the bird.

'It seems my key has gone.' He snatched the bird from his belt, then cried out, dropping it on the raft.

'What –?' He held up his hand. It dripped with blood where the sharp beak had pierced his fingers.

Moss dived for the silver bird, whipping it up by its taloned feet. The ragged man licked his hand.

Salter, still clutching his eye, threw himself in front of Moss.

'Get away from us, you devil.'

'Ah. The foul-mouthed boy come to the rescue of the little sneaker. How touching.'

Before Salter could reply, the raft pitched forward.

In front of them the river began to spin. A whirlpool, deep and furious, carved its way down into the river. An endless swirling tunnel that looked strong enough to suck the sky down with it.

The raft lurched away from the edge of the whirlpool, throwing the ragged man on to his back and Moss beside him. Quick as a whip, she held the beak of the bird to his throat. The tip of the beak pricked his skin. A bubble of black blood oozed out, a worm sliding down his neck.

The ragged man's brittle laugh grated over the water.

'What, you think you can stop me with your toy?'

Before he could say another word, Moss's hand whipped back. There was a flash of silver. With a movement, brief like the flit of a moth's wing, she slashed at the string hanging from his belt. There was a snapping sound and a chink of coins.

336

In Moss's raised hand was the pouch of gold. The smile vanished from the ragged man's face.

'Give that to me, sneaker.'

Moss scrabbled backwards.

'Give it to me, I said.' He began to crawl towards her. 'Or I will teach you the true meaning of pain.'

Moss wobbled to her feet. 'If you want it,' she said, 'then you'll have to fetch it!'

She drew back her hand and flung the pouch high into the air. The ragged man's eyes went with it. For a moment the pouch seemed to hang over them. His hands went up, grasping towards the sky. The pouch began to fall. The ragged man reached out, his fingertips clutching at thin air, the pouch tumbling beyond his reach. And as it fell, he lunged, his bent body falling with it now, grappling for his gold. His scaly hands closed round the bag.

Then there was a scream. A mighty splash. The angry water churned like a millwheel. It was a desperate sight. The ragged man clawing the water helplessly with one hand, the pouch of gold in the other. Then his foot caught the lip of the spinning vortex and his cries became bubbles as his body was snatched by the suck of the whirlpool.

Moss and Salter watched helplessly as the swirling water blurred into a haze of green and black. The water closed in, twisting down and down, until the ragged man was no more than a smear.

'Look!' said Salter.

Lightning fingers of frost were forking across the river. Closing in around the whirlpool. Cricking and cracking until the sides of the whirlpool had crusted to thick ice. For a moment the river seemed to stop.

Moss's heart caught in her throat. Through the ice a dark shape circled.

'Get back!' yelled Salter.

Then the ice exploded. Crashing through the frozen whirlpool was the Riverwitch, her torn dress coiling around her body. Fronds of skin laced across her skull-face. Where her lips had been, now there were none. Just bare bone. Teeth jagged, stretched into an expression Moss could not place.

'Great Harry's pussin ulcers,' breathed Salter.

The raft rocked in the swell of broken ice and around it circled the Riverwitch, her eyes devouring Moss. From the glass-black depths her hands floated upwards. Riverweed trailed from her bone-arms.

'Twelve years,' said the Riverwitch. 'To this very day.' Her voice was thin, stretching out to Moss like cobweb. 'The bargain was made, you see.' Her jagged teeth parted into a hideous grin. 'Bitter is the soul that gave life to this rotting body. But I keep my promises.'

The Witch reached out her arms to Moss. 'River daughter . . .'

'No!' shouted Salter. 'Get away from her!'

'Wait!' said Moss. 'Salter, wait.'

The Riverwitch's candle eyes flickered. Moss could not help but stare back. Into her head drifted the Witch's words from the banks of the frozen river at Hampton.

I call them, but they never come to me.

She held the Witch's gaze.

'I do not mean for them to drown, but they struggle so . . .' Moss realised she'd said those words aloud.

The bitter brightness seemed to vanish from the Witch's eyes. Something like tears mixed with the flame. And Moss saw their reflection, pools of sadness in the black river.

What do you want from me?

What every mother wants from their child.

In that moment, Moss felt the arms of her mother. Holding her baby for the first time. And the arms of Pa, wrapping them both tight. Words whispered soft in her hair. She saw the miller's daughter, wailing as her own child was taken. The last time she would feel her son's embrace.

The Riverwitch held her arms out to Moss.

That was what she wanted.

Moss took a step towards her.

'NO!' cried Salter.

Too late.

Moss stepped off the raft and fell.

She felt the cold bone of the Riverwitch's arms close round her, clasping her. Felt her skull-face against her cheek. Felt the Witch drag her under. Down, into the dark river. Where there was no way back. Riverweed swirled round them, suffocating her, binding them tight.

Moss did not struggle.

She wrapped her warm arms round that torn body. She held the Riverwitch, as the Witch's own child would have held her. As if she were her own mother.

What every mother wants from her child.

To love. To be loved. To be held tight.

Moss held her tight. The warmth of a child's embrace to thaw a Witch's cold heart.

The last thing Moss remembered were two thin hands, holding her face, crying strange green tears that mixed with the ink-black river. Then she passed into darkness.

CHAPTER TWENTY-SIX
Friends

O n the raft, Salter lay on his back. His chest heaved, gasping out great howls. And when his lungs were empty, he simply stared at the sky.

The grey clouds rolled past. Clouds, wind, river, same as always. But nothing would ever be the same.

He closed his eyes. He heard the slap of waves against the raft. He wouldn't fight it. The river could do whatever it wanted. He would drift. Wherever the current took him. It didn't matter now.

An explosion of bubbles shattered the stillness.

Salter's eyes snapped open and he rolled to his knees.

Ten feet from where he drifted, the water was churning, as though pushed by some great force below. Through the froth erupted a bundle of cloth. And as the foam fizzed away, he saw that the bundle had arms and legs and was floundering in the water. And through the spluttering and choking he heard a cry.

Salter didn't need to be called twice. He dived into the river, splashing madly towards her.

'Leatherboots!' he gasped, dragging and heaving the wet body on to the raft.

Moss flopped on to her back, her lips spitting frothy riverwater.

Leaning over her was a boy, his face crunched up with worry. She felt his hands pull the wet hair from her eyes. She opened her mouth to say something, but no words came.

'It's all right.' The boy's voice choked in his throat. 'Should have known you'd be good fer nothin but a boatful of sick.'

'*She let me go,*' whispered Moss. '*I gave her what she had craved all this time. And she let me go.*'

She felt the boy's hand on hers. She saw his eyes crinkle. She saw his smudge-face smiling at her. The smile of her friend Salter.

'Wake up now, Leatherboots. We're here.'

Moss sat up. It was dusk. It had taken just a day to row upriver. The boat that Salter had borrowed was sleeker and faster than his own.

'I never asked,' said Moss. 'Did the person you *borrowed* it from know you were borrowing it?'

'Do you really want to know? Anyway, it got us here quick, didn't it?'

Moss nodded. 'It did . . . thank you.' She hadn't meant for Salter to steal a boat, but she could see there just wasn't any other way. 'We'll give it back.'

'If you like.'

344

'As soon as . . . as soon as we've found him.'

Salter steered the boat to the bank and looped the rope over a tree branch.

'Want me to come?'

Moss shook her head and clambered out of the boat.

The Hampton Wheel was a silhouette against the setting sun. It was the only place left she could think of to look for Pa. Somewhere he might have come to search for her. Moss's heart was tight inside her chest. This place was her last hope.

She set off towards it along the muddy bend of the riverbank.

After Salter had hauled her from the river, he'd taken her to his shack. He'd tried to make her lie down and sleep, but she refused and in the end Salter had given up, realising she wouldn't rest until she had found Pa.

They'd spent the remainder of the day scouring the shore, asking anyone they could. No one had seen him. So she'd persuaded Salter to row her to Hampton and to do it quick. An hour later, he'd returned with the boat.

Please be here, Pa.

It was only a short walk round the river bend, but Moss's legs were strangely weak. She felt the chill of the winter wind, humming through the ruins. The crooked chimney, the tumble of grey stone, all was just as it had been that night in the snow. She forced herself on, stumbling through the fallen rubble.

Be here, Pa.

There was the wheel, joints creaking, shattered paddles scraping the water.

And there next to it was a bundle. A huddle of cloth and limbs. Quite still. A great bear-frame, unmoving in the mud.

'Pa!' Moss ran towards him and fell on his back, shaking his shoulders to try and wake him.

'Pa! Wake up, Pa!'

He did not move. She knelt beside him. 'Pa, wake up. Please wake up!'

She held his face in her hands. His skin was death-grey. But it was warm.

'Pa . . .'

His eyes stayed shut.

She grasped an arm and with great difficulty hauled him upright so he sat, slumped, against a block of fallen wall. His face was a husk, the life sucked out. Lips dry. as though he hadn't had a drink of water for days.

Moss leant into the river and cupped a handful of water to Pa's mouth.

'Pa, you have to drink.'

His eyelids fluttered. He dipped his head and the water ran down his chin.

'You came back,' he said, although his voice was barely a croak. 'I thought you had gone.'

She reached into her pocket for the bread she had brought. Scooping another handful of water from the river, she dipped the bread in it and put it to Pa's mouth.

'Pa, please.'

His parched lips sucked on the soft bread. He tried to swallow and his throat erupted in a spasm of coughing.

'When you left,' he croaked, 'I thought I'd lost you.'

She felt his hand touch hers.

'Pa, I'm sorry. I'm so sorry I ran away.'

'No.' Pa lifted his head a little. 'It was wrong of me to keep you locked in that place.'

'I understand, Pa. You just wanted to keep me safe.'

'I promised your mother.' Pa's eyes searched hers.

'You don't have to worry any more. It's over . . .' She hesitated. The Riverwitch had let her go. Would he believe her?

The wheel creaked and cricked.

'When I came here,' said Moss, 'I wanted to find . . . I don't know, something. Something of mine. A memory, I guess. Of my birth. Of Ma.'

Pa rested his head back against the wall and sighed.

'But I didn't find Ma,' said Moss. 'What I found . . . was you.'

She put down the bread and took his hands in hers. 'I have *you*, Pa. And there couldn't *be* a better father. I couldn't have had a better pa.'

She'd seen him cry only once before and the sight had made her want to turn away. This time she held his gaze and wiped the tears from his cheek with the sleeve of her dress.

She knew what his tears meant. He understood her. He loved her. And one day, if he had to, he would let her go.

She buried her head in his chest. He kissed her hair.

She felt his arms wrap her tight. And he whispered something. She wasn't sure what. But she felt him hug her tighter.

CHAPTER TWENTY-SEVEN
Bluebell Woods

Pa would always be nervous of rivers. It was a different river now of course. Not the roaring Thames. But still, it made Pa nervous.

Moss was watching him tap out the yellow-hot horseshoe. It took him longer than it used to. His hands had become frail and he stooped a little when he walked. All the same, here in the forge he seemed content. This was their home now. Three days' walk from London and a world away from the heaving city. They'd been in the village just a few months, but word had spread that the new blacksmith shod a horse with skill and always asked a fair price. And those who came to the forge noticed how the blacksmith's daughter delighted in the simplest things. Running barefoot in the grass and climbing tall trees, even if she did seem a little old for all that.

They didn't really know what to make of the gutter-mouthed boy that lived with them. At dawn he'd fish the chalk river in a boat he'd made himself, throwing fat trout from his nets into the hands of the village children. The rest of the day he spent in the forge, working the bellows, mending the tools, holding the horses for the smith. And although some said they thought he'd make a fine blacksmith himself one day, others shook their heads and said he had the look of a boy who'd steal the laces from your boots when you weren't looking.

'Pa?'

'Mmm?' Pa didn't look up, lost in the *chink-chink* of his hammer.

'It's today, isn't it?'

He stopped chinking and dunked the horseshoe in a bucket of water. The forge fizzed with steam.

'Yes, Moss. It is today.'

Her hand went to the silver bird tucked in her pocket, where she always kept it now. 'Do you . . . do you think they will do it on Tower Hill?'

'No, I don't think they will do it there,' said Pa gently. 'They will keep her close. Within the Tower walls.'

'Because . . . because . . .'

'Because she is a Queen of England. And whatever people say about her, she deserves a quiet and dignified death.'

News from London often took many days to reach the village. But the day Anne Boleyn had been taken to the Tower, the news had travelled fast. How the Queen was to be tried for treason, her stone-eyed uncle to conduct the trial. And when the trial was over, the verdict travelled just as swiftly. Guilty. As a rat in a grain sack.

So this was the end of the Queen's great adventure, thought Moss.

She shivered. At least it wasn't Pa who would do it. The villagers said there was a Frenchman. An Executioner from Calais, skilled with a sword. They said that if he did his job, the Queen would not know life from death. It would be done in the blink of an eye. A good death, they said. The blink of an eye and her head in a basket on Tower Green.

'Pa . . .'

'Yes?'

'Does the King really want her to die? How is that possible, Pa? I mean, if he loved her once?'

'Do you think he did?'

'I *know* he did.'

Moss traced her finger down one of the iron-headed hammers that hung from the forge wall. 'Do you . . . do you ever think about our days back then?'

'I try not to, Moss. We are far away now. We must try to let those memories slip away. And make new, better memories, to take the place of the old.'

Moss wrapped her arms tight round Pa.

'When the time comes for the Queen, I hope they are right, Pa. I hope that it is quick.'

'I believe it will be,' said Pa.

She remembered the Queen's bright berry eyes, full of mischief. *You can make your way in this world,* thought Moss, *but none of us can predict how or where it will end.*

She thought back to the day she'd escaped from the Tower. So much had changed. She'd found the freedom she'd craved. She'd made friends with a thief and risked her life to save him. She'd gone looking for her mother's love, but found her father's instead. *Hold on to love,* the Queen had said. *Wherever you can find it. Do not let it go.* Pa had always loved her. She knew that now. But she'd needed to find it out for herself.

Moss squeezed Pa tight and felt his gentle arms hug her back.

'Did you know,' he said, 'there are bluebells out in the West Woods?'

'Yes,' said Moss. 'I never saw anything so beautiful. A river of flowers running through the trees.'

Slivers of dusty light stretched across the forge floor. Moss could hear Salter outside. He had promised to row up the river to a shallow pool and teach her to swim.

She pushed open the door. After the darkness of the forge, she blinked in the glare of early summer sun that spread across the fields.

'There you are.'

'Can't get rid of me that easily, shore girl.'

'Wouldn't dream of it. I saved your life, didn't I?'

'Well, the way I remember it, I saved yours at least twice.'

'Saved me in order to rob me, you mean.'

'Great Harry's gout balls, that's all the thanks I get? Can't think why I bothered. You've been more trouble than a hoseful of ferrets!'

Salter's grin spilt from his mouth. His face lit up

and its brightness reached into Moss's heart.

'You ready?' he said.

'To the river,' said Moss.

'To the river,' said Salter.

'Let's go then,' said Moss, and before he could protest she took his hand.

They turned and walked across the green field. And when they got to the riverbank, Moss drank in the sight of the calm water that raked the river bed. Trailing tendrils of water crowfoot swaying to the rhythm of the current. This was a gentle river. Impossibly clear. A river so perfect, it almost made her long for the murky swill of the Thames. As her gaze drifted, she caught a movement, under the surface. A shadow curling under the bank. Too big for a fish. She blinked and stared hard, but it was gone.

The river sparkled, winding its way through the fields. A ribbon of silver that vanished where it met the sky.

A note from the author

This story came from my imagination. It is set in one of England's most compelling historical times, weaving real people, events and places into the lives of my fictional characters. I've tried to stay faithful to what we know of Tudor life and I hope I've managed to conjure some of the feel and the smell and the taste of the period. But it *is* a story. I have made things up.

Much of the inspiration for the book comes from real settings – places alive with stories of their own – the Tower of London, the banks of the River Thames and Hampton Court Palace. I would urge anyone who has the chance, to go and see these places for themselves. We are lucky to have them.

Jane Hardstaff

Acknowledgements

I would like to thank my astounding agent Gillie Russell whose wisdom I depend upon and who got to the heart of the story when it mattered the most; Stella Paskins at Egmont whose editorial brilliance kept the writing alive and made a better book; creators of Undiscovered Voices Sara Grant and Sara O'Connor, and their co-editors Karen Ball and Elizabeth Galloway who have given so many new writers a chance; my New Zealand nieces Martha and Ellie – Martha who asked great questions at a crucial time and Ellie whose quizzical expressions made me rethink; my quietly inspirational parents who have always tried to make things possible; spirited Frea who loves stories and has a wild imagination of her very own; and Nick who has given many wise thoughts, but also time and love. I couldn't wish for more.